Hanson

THE ENGLISH DRAGON BOOK 3

KATHI S. BARTON

This is a work of fiction. Names, characters, places, and incidents are products of the author's imagination or are used fictitiously and are not to be construed as real. Any resemblance to actual events, locations, organizations, or persons, living or dead, is entirely coincidental.

World Castle Publishing, LLC
Pensacola, Florida
Copyright © Kathi S. Barton 2017
Paperback ISBN: 9781629898001
eBook ISBN: 9781629898018
First Edition World Castle Publishing, LLC, September 18, 2017
http://www.worldcastlepublishing.com
Licensing Notes
Cover: Karen Fuller
Editor: Maxine Bringenberg

Chapter 1

Quinn decided that if she ever woke up from this dream, she was going to be terribly upset with someone. She was in a real castle with servants and everything. As she made her way down the stairs again, trying hard not to make any noises that would bring someone after her, she thought of her sister, Carmine, who would be celebrating her tenth birthday in a few months, and how much fun she was having.

Just yesterday she'd been swimming in the big pool of water. Kendrick said she'd been having so much fun that she hated to have her come in for dinner. And Carmine said that the water was warm, not at all like a bath, it was better. It was wonderful seeing her smile again.

"You really should listen to the doctor, my dear." Quinn turned and looked at Elissa, Danburn's mom, when she spoke. "I know how it is, however. I so love to keep moving too. Where are you headed? I'll come with you, as a helper."

"To the window. Carmine said it was snowing and I wanted to see it." Elissa nodded and walked with her, not telling her continually to be careful. "Kendrick is out and so is

Danburn. I think they went to go Christmas shopping."

"They did. I talked with her a little while ago. And she got news that one of Danburn's friends is coming in tonight. You'll like Hanson. He's a nice man." Pausing to rest, Quinn leaned against the banister to get her breath back. "How's your mom today?"

That hurt her. Not the question, but the fact that she would have to tell her that her mom was dying. Looking at the window, wanting to change the subject, she thought of life without her mom. But being a realist was what got her through things, so she answered Elissa.

"She isn't going to make it much longer, I'm afraid. I've known that for some time, but the stress of me being hurt and my sister sick has taken its toll on her. She's...My mom is special to me, and she's all I have besides my little sister." Elissa said she was sorry. "I am as well. She's trying to be strong, but I think that's making it harder for her. I told her a little while ago just to let go. I hate it, but I can't handle seeing her suffering much more."

Quinn saw her mom every chance she got. But she also noticed that while she was in the room with her, her mom didn't rest as well. Fussing at her for getting up, or worrying after her and Carmine. After assuring her that they were both well and Carmine was no longer ill, her mom closed her eyes with a smile and she'd left her there.

"She's comfortable though, isn't she?" Quinn said that she was. The medications were helping her a great deal. "I lost my husband. He got an infection from a shard of iron we didn't know that he had and it killed him. You'd think that it only happened yesterday the way I feel some days. But I miss him every day."

They started walking again, and just as they were going

to the front of the house, her sister came running around the corner. Carmine was the picture of health, and it made Quinn smile every time she saw her.

"Did you know that I have a snow coat? And boots? Kendrick gave them to me. She said that it's a present with no ties. I didn't know what she meant, so Danburn told me that it was just a present, without being something for my birthday or Christmas." Quinn told her that was wonderful. "I'm going to miss them when we go."

After Carmine left them to run more, Elissa asked her if they were going somewhere. She smiled at the older woman. They were the kindest people she'd ever known. Nodding, she sat down on the chair that had been moved near the front window for her.

"We can't stay here forever. I mean, I have to get myself a job and a place to stay." She had lost her job, but thanks to the state, she wasn't going to have to work nearly as many jobs to keep them in food and meds. "Rett said that he was looking into a few things for me. I don't know what that means, but he told me to leave it to him."

"I would imagine that he does have a handle on things. He's a good man too. And happy. There was a time when he was as sad as any man I've ever known. Cassie has done him a world of good." Quinn said she liked her too. "I do as well. I've always thought of Rett as my son, and now that he's living close to us, I can go and see him whenever I wish. The rest of them too. I think that all of them, for the most part, have decided to stay here. Or at least have a home that they can come to when they need to be with family. But as for you leaving, I don't think that Kendrick has any idea of your plans, does she?"

"She can be pretty bossy, can't she?" They both laughed.

"No, I've not told her. I think she's figured it out that I'm needing to go, but she won't be as easy to convince of it. I've loved staying here for the last two weeks, but it's time we got back up on our own two feet. I need to get Carmine into some kind of school. And then there is the rest of our lives. Things haven't been all that good for us."

Elissa sat down next to her on the little couch that had been brought for her as well. To have someone know your every need and take care of it, to not have to go without because you have all the money in the world, was amazing. It wasn't anything she thought she could get used to, not even in several lifetimes.

"Have Danburn and Kendrick spoken to you yet?" Quinn shook her head, bracing for the bad news. "They will. There are things that you need to be made aware of. And things you need to understand. I think their plan was for them to speak to you this evening. After your sister goes to bed."

"Do we need to start packing now? I've been just living out of my suitcase—not that I have that much—in case they get tired of us. Carmine isn't so easy to keep neat...that's it, isn't it? We'll go, but I really do need to—" The hand over her mouth shut her up. "I'm sorry. I just worry."

"No, nothing to be sorry for or to worry about. You'll be fine." A noise, or the lack of it, had the two of them turning to the grand staircase. It wasn't until she saw the doctor, Pierce, go running up the stairs that she knew it was her mom. Standing up, she turned when Elissa told her to wait. "I'll go up now, but you take your time, child. Hurrying up there will get you hurt or worse. I won't tell you to stay here, but don't hurt yourself."

She was gone. Her mom, she knew, had died. Moving toward the stairs, she was stopped when the doorbell rang.

Quinn stood there, not wanting to go and needing to at the same time, but turned to the door. She opened it just as a man turned away to speak to someone behind him.

"I can get them. Just leave them there and I'll make a couple of trips. No big deal." The man moved as if he was going to get whatever it was now, and she heard Elissa coming back down the stairs.

"Excuse me, but I'm going to leave the door open for you. I have to go upstairs. My mom is...I have to go upstairs." He looked at her then and she felt her heart flutter. Good Lord, he was handsome. "I'm so sorry. Please, I have to go."

"Let me help you. I can smell your pain." That wasn't right, so she was sure she'd misheard him. "Come on, love. Let me help you out and you'll be fine."

He picked her up like she weighed nothing at all and carried her to the stairs. It was strange and delightful to be handled like this. But before they made it up even three of the stairs, Elissa stopped them.

"I'm so sorry, Quinn." It was true then; her mom was really gone. Sobbing, she buried her face in the neck of the man who held her. "Hanson, take her on up, please. Her mother has just passed. And do be careful, son. She's been hurt badly herself."

Quinn had no idea how they made it the rest of the way to her mom's room. Before she knew it, she was in the large room and sitting by her side. Holding her hand, Quinn told her mom how sorry she was and that she wished she'd been there for her. All the while, the man, Hanson, stayed with her. Carmine came in a few minutes later and tried to sit on her lap.

"Here you go, honey. Come sit with me. I'll hold you up." Carmine, usually so reserved around strangers, went right to

Hanson and climbed onto his lap. Holding her gently, Hanson told her how sorry he was and that he had her. They both cried for several minutes before Pierce came in to talk to her.

"I'm so sorry, Quinn. But I will tell you that after you talked to her earlier, she did rest easier. Telling her that you were going to take care of Carmine, that helped." Quinn told him of course, it was her sister. "Yes, but at times like this, you have no idea how the smallest things can seem so large when you're ill. I'm to understand that she wanted to be cremated, correct?"

"Yes. She thought that her ashes could be placed with my dad's. He's been cremated as well." Pierce nodded. "Was she in any pain? I mean, I should have been here. I was only going to.... She sent me to see the snow."

"No, she wasn't in any pain. The medications were helping her with that. She simply went to sleep and that was all." She nodded, holding her mom's hand while he continued. "Danburn and Kendrick are on their way back. As soon as they get here, we'll call the ambulance to take her to the funeral home."

Hanson and Pierce talked quietly. Carmine left them when the maid from the kitchen came to get her. She was going to enjoy some cookies and milk, Carmine told her. As soon as her sister was out of earshot, Quinn laid her head on her mom's chest and spoke to her.

"I'm going to miss you so much. I'm so glad that you were here instead of the hospital. You would have hated that. And they wouldn't have let you rest as well, either. I love you, Mom. So very much." Crying again, she felt someone put their hand on her back and looked up at Hanson. "She'd been sick for so long. They told her that she'd have six months, tops, but she didn't even get to have three. And now she's missed

Thanksgiving too. What am I going to do without her now?"

He got down on his knees and held her to him. It was strange to think that though she didn't know this man, she felt so at home in his arms. As she let tears fall over her cheeks, she had a fleeting thought of how it would feel to have someone hold her like this all the time. But men like this one, rich and probably famous also, wouldn't ever think to do this if she'd not been in such need.

"I'm all right now." Pulling away from his arms was the most difficult thing she'd had to do in a while. "I'm okay now. I'm sure you didn't come here to help me out. I heard you were coming. I thank you for what you've done for us, but I'm sure this wasn't part of your planned visit."

"Its fine, my dear. And yes, Danburn invited me for a holiday. However, I had no idea that things were going to go so well for me when I got here. To get to hold a pretty woman in my arms and be her knight in shining armor isn't something that a man gets to do often." She nodded and told him he was being kind. "No, not kind, truthful. My name is Hanson McClain. You're...?"

"Quinn Langley. My sister is Carmine Langley. We're cousins to Kendrick. Well, not really. My mom was good friends with Kendrick's father's family, and we sort of grew up together. As much as we could." He said that he'd heard about Kendrick's mom. "Yeah, not a nice person. I lost track of Kendrick after she was hurt, but she called me when I was shot and came to get me. Who would have thought that we only lived a drive away? Like decades hadn't passed."

"That's the way it is with the Englishes. But my parents aren't all that nice either. In fact, they're a pain in my ass. Not nice people at all. Thankfully, Danburn would bring me here when things got too bad, and I'd hang out with his family.

11

I've thought of Elissa as my mom since I was a child." She nodded. "You're very beautiful, has anyone told you that?"

"Right. No, they haven't. You're a nice man, and a flirt. But you don't have to do that." He asked her what he'd done. "Being nice. I thank you for bringing me up here. I hope you didn't hurt your back. I'm not exactly a lightweight."

"You don't weigh anything to me. Especially since I'm not—" Elissa cleared her throat, then shook her head. "Ah, so you've not been told. All right. Then we'll talk later. Elissa, my love, how have you been?"

Quinn had no idea what was going on, but it didn't matter. She had to make arrangements, then find a place for her and Carmine to live. As Elissa and Hanson spoke, she thought of all she had to take care of, and soon. Her mom had left her. But she was also in a better place, a place without pain. And that, she knew, was the point of her leaving her all alone in the world.

~~~

Hanson sat in his friend's office while he made arrangements to have the body picked up. There wasn't anything for Hanson to do to help him, so he thought about what had brought him here. Certainly not the little woman upstairs, that's for sure. But he was here, and so was she. While the timing could have been a lot better, he wasn't sure what he was supposed to do now. But he'd hold his secret with him just a little while longer.

Danburn hung up just as Hanson was going to leave him. "I'm sorry to have you sit there bored, but things had to be taken care of. The poor woman has been ill for a long time. I mean, in human years at least. By the time we got them here, Madeline was so far gone that we weren't able to do anything but make her comfortable. It's sad, really. The way

12

that she just gave up toward the end. Pierce said that had she had better care in the beginning, she might have been able to live a little longer, but they could only do so much. They were on all kinds of government programs that did little to nothing for her." Hanson told him he was sorry. "Not exactly the homecoming that I wanted you to have."

"It's fine, Danburn. I'm all right." He stood up. "I have luggage to take someplace. I'm assuming that since you already have a full house, I should—"

"You will stay here." Hanson nodded and sat back down when Danburn asked him to. He could have argued about the hotel, but it would have done no good. Danburn's word was law where he was concerned. "We'll get this cleared up and then have a nice dinner. I'm sure that Quinn won't be joining us. I had hoped that you'd hit it off, but we'll get through this, and then the two of you can become friends too. She's a wonderful person. You and her, you have a lot in common too, I think."

He hoped they hit it off too, now that he knew what she was to him. Sitting there while he thought of his mate upstairs, he also thought of his parents. They were going to be very unhappy with him, and would absolutely hate Quinn. If for no other reason than she was his mate. There were things—

"Hanson? Where did you go just now?" He felt embarrassed and smiled. "There it is, that famous smile that got you out of more trouble than anyone I knew. I'm glad that you're here. With Thanksgiving in a few days, I think it'll be great. Kip and the rest of the gang are coming too. They should all three arrive tomorrow sometime."

"The girl and her mom, what's up with them? I know that she's sort of related, though not by blood, to Kendrick, but why was the older daughter, I think her name is Quinn, shot?" Danburn leaned back in his chair and regarded him. It was a look he'd seen on the dragon king a million times. Too knowing and too smart. "What do you have running through that thick skull of yours?"

"She doesn't know what we are yet. We thought it best that we waited, to see how things went. She's your mate, isn't she?" He nodded, his heart feeling the push of happiness right then. "We have talked to her, but Kendrick was watching the news one night and heard about it. Quinn was applying for aid from the state for some help for her mom and sister. The poor girl was working three or four jobs, trying her best to make it, but the meds were too much for her and her mom needed them. While there, an employee had a breakdown, and shot Quinn three times while she tried to protect some children that were there. And another woman — Smith, I think her name was — the mother of the four kids, was also killed. Then the employee, CarolAnn Bishop, put the gun to her head and killed herself before the police arrived. It was touch and go for a while whether or not Quinn was going to be able to come here, what with her injuries and how much pain she was in. But Kendrick, as is her way, pushed and pushed until she was released to Pierce's care."

"And then your lovely wife brought them all here and has been taking care of them, correct?" He said that was pretty much it. "Now the mom is gone, leaving a little sister and my mate.... Where do they have to go now? Besides with me."

"Rett is an attorney, as you know, and he's working on getting them representation for some money. He can't do it himself, sadly, because he's our mayor, but he knows some people that can. Also, while talking about him, his mom is in jail and his dad is out. That's another long story, but I think you'll enjoy that one." Hanson laughed but still thought of

14

Quinn. "You upset? About any of this? The girl, her sister? I should tell you, Hanson, they've been dealt some pretty shitty hands. Not just with this, but in looking into their lives, it's been pretty much a downhill shit ball from the beginning."

"My parents will hate them both." Danburn nodded. "As for the little girl, no, I don't mind having her in my life too. Our life, I suppose I should say now. And as you called it, my parents have decided that now the house is paid off and taxes caught up, they can come back. I've not seen them yet, and I have no desire to, but I've given word that they're not to enter the castle, nor are they to touch the money in my account. I'm sure if they don't know where I am yet, they'll figure it out soon enough. And I have to tell you, that worries me a great deal. They'll hurt her, just to get back at me."

"Let them come. We can take care of them." Hanson knew that he'd say that and told him it was his fight. "No. You're one of my best friends, a man that I have come to love like a brother. It's our fight. And I'm sure we can make them rue the day they messed with us."

"Your mom will have fun with it." They both laughed and were still doing so when Elissa came into the room. After hugging her tightly, they all made their way into the living room to talk. Quinn and her sister were in there and started to leave when they entered. "Please, don't leave on our account. We were just going to talk about Thanksgiving."

"My sister is ready for bed, I'm afraid. And she's had a rough day. So, if you'll excuse me, I'm going to go up with her." He and Danburn stood when she did, and he could tell that she was embarrassed. "Good night." Then she was gone, taking a small part of his heart with him. Soon enough, she'd have it all, and he was glad to give it to her.

Elissa eyed him strangely but didn't ask. He was sure

she'd figure it out soon. Danburn laughed, and he knew that she'd been told by him. And Elissa, being Elissa, surely made a comment along the lines of it was about time. He loved this family, and had always thought of them as a better family than the one he was born to. Elissa had been the mother that he'd always needed, and Danburn and the others, brothers.

"I've been thinking, I need a safe house for.... I need a safe house until my parents see the light." Danburn asked him if here was all right. "It might be, but I'd rather not. I don't want you to be involved in this thing with them. I know you will be...they'll blame whatever I'm doing on you, as you know. But I would like to have a place that they can focus their anger on me and not you. I know it's going to be bad, and to be honest, I just want it over with. Especially now."

"Your parents, you mean?" He nodded at Elissa. "They should have been dealt with a great many decades ago. They need to be horsewhipped, or worse. What have they done now, Hanson? Something diabolical, I'm betting."

"They left me with a mess. I had called the bank on another matter, and since the banker knows me, he told me about the taxes as well as the lack of upkeep on the house. My God, you should have seen it. The animals that roam the ground were all but dead. It took me over a month to get that alone squared away. Then there were the taxes. Fifty-two years of back taxes. I had to sell off some of the family things just to get it taken care of that day. Money wasn't something that I had readily, but I do now. I've since been able to get the things back, but you have no idea what kind of mess the home was in. Even the staff...There wasn't any money for them to fall back on after my parents left them there holding the bag. Most of them had begun sleeping in the keep to have a place to go at night, and to keep out the town." Elissa told him she was sorry. "Not as sorry as they're going to be when I see them. I've had enough. It's been difficult enough trying to get things finished up without them being childish, as well as a couple of deadbeats. And there was Jessie…. They left her there, Danburn. Just left her to die all alone. I had no idea."

"You should have called me. I would have helped you." Hanson knew that, and it was precisely the reason that he hadn't called. Not that he was embarrassed, because Danburn knew his family almost as well as he did, but he just didn't want to bother his friend. Again. "Well, you're here now and we can take care that they don't get in. I insist that you allow me to let someone go in there and keep an eye on it. I need to help you."

"You make sure that things here are safe too. You know what they're going to do. And now with Quinn in the picture, I don't want her hurt either." He stood up when he heard someone coming. Her scent blew toward him and he knew it was going to be her. When she entered the room, he could tell she'd been crying again.

"I'm sorry to interrupt your visit, but I wanted to ask you about the arrangements. I should have done so earlier, but my mind wasn't clear." Danburn asked her to have a seat and she did. "I seem to be in a fog right now, but I know that things have to be taken care of before we leave."

"You're leaving?" She looked at Hanson as he glanced at Danburn. "You're not kicking her to the curb, are you, old man? I thought for sure you were going to open your home to all that needed you. Sort of a home for wayward friends."

"I didn't need him." He wanted to smile at her tone…so indignant, and hot mad. He loved it. "His wife came to get me and brought me here when I was out of it. I'm pretty sure that if I was forced to come here, I might have remembered

17

that. Who are you anyway to ask such a thing of Danburn and his wife? They've been nothing but kind to us in our hour of need."

As if she realized what she'd done, gotten upset at a stranger, she looked at Danburn and he could tell that she was going to cry. Getting up, Hanson pulled her from her chair and held her while she did. Danburn and his mom left them, closing the door behind them.

"There now, it's all right. I have you." He wasn't sure what to say to her, so he started talking about his mom and dad. "You should meet my parents. You will eventually, but let me warn you now, they're not nice. I mean, on a scale of one to ten, ten being the worst they could be, they'd be upwards of about ten million. And my mom? Well, let's just say that she gives a whole new meaning to the word bitch. My dad...he's not much better. What is it you call a male version of bitch?"

"Bastard, I guess. Why do you think I'll meet them?" He shrugged and brushed her wet hair from her cheeks. "I'm sorry that I snapped at you. I don't normally do that sort of thing to someone I don't know. Perhaps you bring out the worst in me."

"Could be. But usually women swoon at my feet." She smiled at him. "Christ, you're beautiful when you smile. I'd love to kiss you."

"Whatever for?" He was shocked by the question, but before he could tell her, she pulled away. It was like being given warmth in his heart to have it taken away. "I'm very sorry for snapping at you. I've had a stressful few weeks. My mom...Well, I guess you know that she passed away. And now my sister and I have to find us a place to stay."

"I don't think you should leave here. I mean, not right away anyway. Danburn was just telling me that he likes having you here. And Carmine is a joy." Not true, but he knew that Danburn would say that if asked. She moved back more and he took a step toward her. "I mean, it's the holidays, and mine and Danburn's friends will be here soon."

"All the more reason for us to get out of your hair. We have...What are you doing? Stop following me." He told her he couldn't help it. "Figure it out. I'm not sure what you think is going on, but you have to stop this. And just because I seemed to fall apart on your shoulder doesn't mean that I'm going to let you kiss me. It's...We're strangers."

"Just one kiss." She was afraid of him, and he could almost taste it. "I'm sorry. I don't see that many pretty girls, and I get lonely."

Instead of laughing, as he had hoped she would, she turned on her heel and left him. Hanson sat down. Then after thinking about what a fool he'd made of himself, he started laughing, which brought in Danburn again. Then he thought of the look on Danburn's face when he told him what he'd done and he laughed harder. It was the best feeling he'd had in a very long time. Now he had to woo his mate back into his arms. He had a feeling it was going to be much more difficult than dealing with his parents.

But a good deal more fun.

Chapter 2

Carmine sat very still and watched the people. There were a lot of them there, and all of them were giants compared to her and her sister. Glancing at the casket that had been closed since she'd arrived, Carmine thought of her mom. She'd been so sick for a very long time, and now she was gone. Looking around for Quinn, she wondered what they were going to do now.

She had an idea that they'd be staying here. It was a lovely house, and she wasn't sick any more. Carmine liked the people that came around, and enjoyed having Elissa there when she needed a hug or a laugh. They were the nicest people she'd ever met, and she knew what they were.

The people, friends of Danburn's from his childhood, had been nice to them since they'd arrived. At first she was afraid of the big man, Danburn, but he was nice and warm, like he was a big blanket rolled up around her. And his friends were nice too. But it was the first man, Hanson, that she liked the most. He was funny, but sad too.

"How you holding up, sweetheart?" She let Mrs. English

hold her hand when she took it into her warm one. "I saw that your sister was doing much better today. It's best to get this sort of thing out of the way, so that way you can start again. It's so sad to lose someone. I know how badly it hurts."

"Mom was sick all the time. I'm glad she's not hurting anymore, but I'm going to miss her very much." Elissa, as she'd asked her to call her, said she missed her husband too. And he'd been gone a long time. "Quinn said we'd have to find us a place to live now. She said we can't be sponging off your good nature anymore."

"You aren't sponging off anyone. And the two of you are welcome to stay for as long as you wish. But if you do move out, I want you to promise me that you'll see me once in a while." Carmine wasn't sure how that was going to work since they didn't have a car, nor did she think that the buses came out here. "If you wish, I can make sure you have our phone numbers when you go. If you go."

"We don't have a phone, and we probably won't for a bit either. We gotta keep a tight belt, Quinn said." She knew what that meant...they were poor. "It's really nice of you to let us heal here. And Quinn said we could stay until Thanksgiving. I love mashed potatoes and turkey."

"We have ham too, with all the trimmings. It's been a good long time since we've celebrated much of anything. With my extra boys here, it's going to be like old times, minus my husband. He so loved the holidays, and those men. But my favorite part of Thanksgiving is the pies. We'll have a variety too. Pumpkin, apple, and cherry, as well as a few traditional ones. I don't care for mincemeat, but that'll be there as well. Have you met the others yet?"

"Yes, I did at breakfast. They're really nice, but Hanson, he looks upset. Like he wants to hurt one of them." Elissa

22

laughed, but Carmine saw nothing funny about the way he was growling at them and being mean. "Is he mad at my sister? He keeps looking at her."

"Mad? No, honey, he's far from mad at her. More like he hasn't any idea what to do with her. And the problem is, he probably doesn't. He's not had such a good role model for this sort of thing." That didn't make any sense to her either, so she kept her mouth shut. "You'll understand soon enough. We'll have a nice celebration tomorrow and we'll have fun. All right?"

"Yes, ma'am." When she got up to leave her, Carmine looked for Quinn again. Making her way to her sister, she put her hand in hers and felt her squeeze her hand just a little tighter. "Are you all right, Quinn?"

"Yes, as good as I can be. How about you? You want me to take you out for a little while? We can walk across the street and get an ice cream if you want." That sounded good to her, so they went to get their jackets. "We can't be too long. I don't know many of these people, but we should be here for them, but I need a break too."

Yesterday a nice lady had come by to take them shopping. Carmine wasn't sure if her sister was upset then too, but they'd gotten nice dresses to wear, and coats. After they got back home—well, to Danburn's castle—she'd found a lot of boxes and bags of clothing in her room that fit her as well. Quinn said that it was too much, but that she really needed them. Carmine decided that she'd take very good care not to get anything on them in case they had to sell them for money. Money, her sister had told her, was going to be very tight for a little while, until she got a job. Carmine wondered if she should have one too, after school let out.

The ice cream shop wasn't all that busy. Carmine knew

what she wanted, a vanilla dish with sprinkles. Before ordering, however, Hanson came to sit with them, and that seemed to make Quinn mad too.

"I came to help you eat whatever you buy. I love ice cream myself, but just the plain for me." Quinn looked pinched and ordered a single dip of her favorite, mint chocolate chip. "I could eat that too. Will you taste like that when you're finished, Quinn?"

"Behave. What is wrong with you? I'm here with my little sister. Behave yourself...or better yet, go away." He winked at Carmine and something occurred to her. Hanson was making her sister mad on purpose. "Carmine, what is it you want, honey?"

After ordering her treat, she watched as Hanson spoke quietly to the waitress. Flirting, she supposed, and understood that less than she did making Quinn mad on purpose. But he had only doubled their order and ordered himself a large vanilla too. Carmine watched the two of them.

Hanson was trying to hold Quinn's hand. And when that didn't work, he asked for a kiss. It was strange to see Quinn so upset with someone. She never got mad at anyone. But when he put his arm behind her, laying it on the chair, Quinn looked at her; apparently ignoring him seemed to be the best way to deal with him. Carmine didn't think that was going to work either. He seemed very determined.

"I've found us two apartments that we can look at after Thursday. One has two bedrooms and the other three. It's much cheaper here than it is at home. I know that it was a few hours away, but it's far enough removed from here that it made a difference. And they're both within walking distance of the local school." Hanson helped the waitress set their orders in front of them, and she stared at the large ice cream.

24

"Carmine, you don't have to eat all that."

"Okay." She wasn't sure she could anyway. In addition to the two big scoops, there was a little bowl of extra sprinkles for it. "You find you a job yet? I've been looking for help wanted signs in windows when I go by them. Maybe you can bake some pies for that restaurant down the street."

"Maybe, but not yet." Hanson asked her what she was looking for. "I've been a receptionist for a doctor before, but I usually wait tables. I'm not sure how much of that I can do yet, but I need a job. And I cooked for the local bakeries when they needed something. I can cook well, but not on the scale that this place has on their menu."

"I could help you, if you'd let me." She shook her head and Hanson looked at Carmine. "Your sister is very stubborn, isn't she? I've offered to buy her a home, pay for a car, and even pay for anything she wants, but she keeps turning me down. If she keeps that up, I might get my feelings hurt. What do you think?"

"My mom said that she's practical. Like she saves and saves for something before she gets it." She ate a bite of her ice cream. "Mom used to just buy her whatever she needed, and she said it cut out the middleman. I'm not sure what that means, but it worked."

"Good idea. What sort of house do you want?" She told him she liked the castle. "I have one too. But it's not close to here. I grew up there. My parents have...well, it's being repaired now, but I used to love it there."

"Why not now?" He said it was complicated. "Which means you think I won't understand. I know a lot of things. I'm not dumb. Like I know that you guys aren't human."

He didn't say anything, and she thought perhaps she'd gotten it wrong and told him she was sorry. Hanson shook his head and told her it was fine. She hoped so. Carmine didn't want to make a non-human mad at her.

"How did you know? I mean, did someone tell you?" Quinn shook her head in response. He turned to Carmine. "You know that I'm not human? How did you figure it out?"

"I don't know. Is it supposed to be a secret?" He told Carmine that it wasn't. "I don't know how I know a lot of things, but I just do. I guess...I don't know, but I could tell that you are very old, like hundreds of years old, like Danburn. I mean, I know a few others too. I don't know what you are, but you aren't human like us."

"No, none of us are. You and your sister, you're the only two that are human at the castle." Quinn didn't ask him what they were, so he didn't say it. But Carmine wanted to know. She had an idea what they were but wasn't sure, since she'd never met a dragon before. "It doesn't bother you? That you're staying with a bunch of paranormals?"

"Should it?" He said no to Quinn's question. Then he looked at Carmine. She wanted to ask him, to have him tell her that he was something big, something that could save them, but she only pushed away her ice cream and said she was full.

As they made their way back across the street, she held his hand and her sister's. It was nice, having someone on both sides of her. Her mom hadn't been able to walk with her for quite a while. By the time they were inside the big building again, where her mom's funeral was being held, she was exhausted. It had been a hard few weeks. Lying down, she simply closed her eyes. She knew that Quinn or one of the others would protect her if she needed it.

~~~

Hanson kept an eye on the two women in his life. Well,

they weren't yet, but they would be soon enough. He also watched the others. Hanson loved them all like brothers, but they were flirting with his mate. He supposed if he told them what she was to him, then they'd back off. Or perhaps not. They could be a pain in the ass more than anyone he knew.

"I just heard." He asked Kip what he'd heard. "That your parents are back causing trouble. Did you know that they're in trouble with the Dragon Board again?"

"Yes. Danburn said he'd talk to them about it, but I don't think it'll do him any good." Kip asked him what he was going to do. "Not get them off, if that's what you're thinking I should do. But no, I'm looking into getting them arrested and taken in. Danburn, as you know, has a great deal more weight in this than I do."

"Yes. While I knew that he was powerful and high up on the food chain, I never knew that he was a duke, did you?" He said that he had, as a matter of fact. And wondered what Kip would think of him being one as well. "His housemate is cute, don't you think? I was going to ask her out."

"Don't." Kip grinned at him. "Who told you? And if so, do you know if they have their last will and testament written out?"

"No one. You've been glaring at us all night. I volunteered to come over and be the one to make sure." Kip turned to the others and gave them a thumbs up. "We'll leave her alone now. Besides, I don't think she was happy with us flirting with her anyway. Sort of a kitten, isn't she?"

"I don't know yet. I mean, since I've known her, she's been hurt and lost her mom. They were really close." He asked about the sister. "She's taken to me now. Not a lot, but as I said, they've been through a great deal. I want to protect them from this, but even I can't take away their pain. I hurt for them both."

"I've been looking around, for houses. Are you planning to stay too?" He said it was up to them. "Good answer. I think they want to. The little one, Carmine, said that she was looking forward to tea with Elissa sometime. And if you ask me, Quinn has the look of someone that could tear you a new ass if she wanted. But she's not found her inner beast yet. Like I said, a kitten, but she has sharp claws ready to do business."

"You think so? I'm not sure. She has shown a little temper when she's pissed at me, but it's hard to tell. I'm worried more about my parents getting to her. There is no telling what they'll do when they find her." He thought about his sister, Jessie. "I don't fear them for myself, but they could hurt her."

"They'll never get to her." He looked at Kip. "Trust me when I tell you, for as much kidding as we've done over this, we'd protect her with our lives. And it would matter very little to any of us if they're our elders or not. They're fucking toast."

"Thank you. We're going to have a talk with her tomorrow, and I just found out that Carmine has some knowledge that we're not human. She guessed, if you can believe that. But she doesn't know what we are. Kendrick said she'd help us." Kip thought that was a good idea. "I don't know how to talk to her, to be honest. I'm slightly afraid of hurting her with my words. I've never been around a good relationship except for the Englishes, and you know my family."

"Yes. May I ask you something?" Hanson nodded, not sure that he wanted him to, really. "Jessie...did they hurt her? I mean, she'd been ill for a little while, but did they kill her?"

"I think so." Kip said nothing, but Hanson could almost feel his mind working. "When I visited her in the fall of her last year, I knew that she was feeling better. Mom said that it

28

was just because I was there, and she was showing off. But Jessie said she was feeling good, so I believed her. And we made plans for her to come and stay with me. It was the last time that I spoke to her face to face."

It wasn't, however, the last time he' spoken to her. A few hours before he'd felt her death, the pain in his heart and soul, he had spoken to her. She told him everything, from the fact that their house was in poor repair, to the Dragon Board looking for their parents. He told her he was coming for her.

It's too late for that, brother dear. I'm nearly gone now. He'd had to sit down, his knees giving out on him. *They've poisoned me, I think. I have no proof, but I can feel it in my blood. They've gone now, left me here to die. I believe that they heard us planning and it pissed them off. Will you do me a favor?*

Anything you wish. Please, hang on, Jessie. I'm coming. She told him again it was too late, she was dying now. *I love you, Jessie. Please, don't die.*

I'm sorry, little brother, but it's time anyway. I want you to find you someone you can love. Have children, little dragons that remind you of us when we were at the English home. Remember those times? When we were children, all we wanted to be? He told her that he did, every day. *Have children for me, Hanson. And be happy. But kill them. I want you to kill our parents for me, for us.*

Then she was gone. Just like that, he was alone in the world but for his friends. Traveling home, he found her just as she said he would. In her bed, alone in the room without food or water. The staff, the few that had been left, had scattered when he arrived, terrified that he would be as bad as his parents. Burying his sister's body, he vowed then that they'd pay. His parents would pay dearly for what they'd done to her and him. Then he'd gotten the call from the bank.

He'd told Danburn a fib, not wanting to share just yet that

he'd come home to find his sister dead in her bed, the house in shambles, as well as the bank at the doors. He'd had to take care of the arrangements for Jessie, take care of the family home, and make repairs on the house so that it was livable again, all done in a matter of months. His heart broken, getting the call from Danburn had been like a lifeline. Something that he'd needed for a very long time.

He sat near Quinn when the services were conducted. Hanson was proud of her, the way she made sure her sister was all right, telling her when she cried that it was all right, that their mom was no longer in pain. And when the service was finished, he escorted her to the car that would take them all back to Danburn's home for some light dinner and comfort. Hanson held her while she sobbed all the way there.

The house was somber. He knew that the staff had been working all afternoon on the meal, and had everything ready when they returned. There were flowers everywhere, planters too. Hanson knew that Danburn had paid for everything, but said it was part of the settlement from the hospital. Madeline would be cremated and then put into an urn with her husband. Then someday, soon he hoped, the two of them would be buried on some land that Quinn and he would buy for themselves. He was looking into that as well, having a home that would be good for the three of them.

It wasn't too late when the villagers left. He was in the living room with everyone else, while Rett was telling them about his mom and her jail sentence. There was another woman that he'd never cared for. Elba Welsh was almost as rotten, if not just a little rottener, than his own mom. And now she was in prison.

"Dad and I are having a wonderful time catching up. He's got his own place, and for the most part stays to himself.

But lately he's been getting out more. And he's found himself a job." Kendrick asked him what he was doing. "Working in a shop with this woman, and they're having a good time there too. I think she was putting it on the market, but Dad convinced her to keep it going, and they go to auctions and such to fill it up. It's good to see him so happy again."

When Rett and Cassie left, Danburn asked him if now was all right with him to talk. Hanson asked him if he thought it was a good time, and he said that it was better now than her finding out on her own. That, he supposed, was a good idea, but he could see his friend's point. Danburn said he'd start.

"We'd like to have a talk with you, Quinn. It's about what we are." She told him again that she knew they weren't human, and Danburn smiled. "We figured you knew that part, but we think it's important that you know what we are. All of us."

"Why is it important? I mean, in a few days I'm going to be leaving here. I have to move on with my life. You were kind enough to take us in when we needed it, but Carmine and I have been here long enough." Danburn looked at Hanson, then Quinn did. "What's going on?"

"If you know that we're not human, then you also know how our counterparts, our mates, work, yes?" She nodded at his question, then looked around the room at the rest of them. "I'm your mate. I've known since I carried you up the stairs that first day. You're my other half, and someone that fills me."

"It doesn't matter, does it? I mean, we've not done anything." Her face reddened. "What I mean is, I know that since we've never done anything, it won't hurt you. I'm flattered, really I am, but I don't have anything to offer you as a mate. Right now, I have less than nothing. Not even a home to shelter me."

"What is it you think you need to offer me, love?" She asked him not to call her that. "But that's what you are to me. My love, my heart."

"Look, it's not like I'm even in the same class as you guys, none of you. And I have to care for my sister now too. We're all we have." Kendrick said that she had them all. "I don't know why this is even an issue. We don't need each other. Not really, do we?"

"I need you. More than I ever thought possible." She was shaking her head when he sat next to her. "I know this is a lot to take in. I get that, but I want you to understand some of this now. My parents, I think you heard a little about them, they'll hurt you when they find out. And they will. Once they can smell that I've found you, they'll do everything in their power to hurt you. Perhaps even try to kill you and Carmine."

"Why? What did I ever do to them? I mean, I've been trying...I don't understand any of this." He understood, and when Elissa sat on her other side, he waited to see what she did. "I should go. I mean, this doesn't concern me, does it?"

"I'm afraid that it does now, dear. You see, unlike other shifters, we're a different breed all together. There is no reason or need for sex, exchanging blood, or other things when one of our kind finds their mate. It's as if some sort of hormone is released. I can smell it on Hanson, as well as you. The process has begun." Quinn asked what process. "You're an immortal, love. Just as the rest of us are. Not your sister, not yet, but she will be when she reaches a certain age. She'll have benefits that will keep her healthy and safe now. It's what we offer to our mates as a provision of us staying with each other."

"What are you all?" No one said a word to her, all of them looking at Hanson. "What are you, Hanson? A monster?

32

Something that is going to terrify me for the rest of my life? What are you?"

"Dragon." She sat there, staring at him for several moments before she stood up. Dana smiled at her when she was close to him. When she asked him what he was, he said the same thing. And all of them did…Griffith, Kip, and Danburn told her they were dragons. "Kendrick isn't, but Cassie is. And the baby that Kendrick now carries is a dragon too. Danburn is the king of dragons, and Kendrick his queen."

"Why are you doing this? Don't you think I've been through enough? I'm glad that you're all immortal. I would imagine that you've been around for a long time, but I'm just me. A woman who is looking after her little sister." Hanson took her hand and led her out to the decking around the house. They all followed them. He knew that showing her would frighten her, but he also knew that she'd have to see to believe. "What are you going to do, change? I can't believe that you're doing this to me."

"Watch." He moved into the yard, knowing that his dragon was large, as big as Danburn's. "He's not a pretty dragon, none of us are. But we aren't monsters, big dragons that could crush a town with a single foot. Never a monster."

He let his dragon consume him. Hanson knew that she was there, he could smell her. But what really surprised him was that he didn't smell fear, not even a little. And when he was fully his beast, he moved slowly toward her and put out his hand for her. He spoke to Danburn, because he knew that she'd not be able to understand him as yet.

"He wants you to trust him. Go into his hand and let him show you that he'd never harm you." Hanson smelled it then, fear and confusion. "He'd never harm you, Quinn. Neither you nor Carmine. You are his."

She put out her hand, but Hanson didn't get his hopes up. If she touched him, it would be more than he'd ever hoped for when he brought her out here. But when her fingers slid over his long claw, he smelled the blood right away. He moved his head lower when she pulled back.

"Let him lick the wound." She shook her head. "It will give you a connection so that he can talk to you. And find you."

"He didn't cut me. I did it." Danburn said he knew that, but if Hanson licked it clean, not only would it heal, but he'd be able to talk to her directly. "I'm not sure about this. It's all so...it's very overwhelming. And he's so big. Like he could smash your house, so big."

She put her hand out and he moved slowly. His tongue was wider than her, his teeth longer than she was tall. And one of his tail scales would weigh as much as, if not more than, she did. But he gently moved his tongue over her wound and tasted her. She was his, and he was in love with her.

Chapter 3

Edwin fell to the ground. His wife, Geraldine, screamed when she too fell. The earth beneath them moved and he felt like his heart had been stabbed. Not a gentle sliding into it, but a hard knock of a blade through and through him. He laid there for several minutes before he sat up on his arse and waited for the earth to stop trembling beneath him. Edwin looked at his mate when she asked him what that was.

"Our son, he's found his mate." Geraldine laughed, hard and long. Edwin didn't find it so funny and told her to shut up. "He's no longer under our control. Now he can do as he pleases."

"He has for many years, Edwin. I don't know why that bothers you so much. So what? He's found a mate. We have the power to take care of her as well. It matters little that he might think we can't, but we both know that together, we're as strong as anything around." She stood and brushed off her clothing. "I don't suppose you know where they might be, do you?"

"Nay, I didn't get that. But they've exchanged blood now.

What on earth do you think he's going to do with a mate? Last we heard, he didn't have anything save a few coins to his name." She said that he'd always been resourceful. And he was. Hanson was never without funds for very long. "Yes, resourceful enough that he's blocked us from our home. What do you suppose he used for that? I didn't think he had any magic save the bit to shift, and of course, to irritate us."

They had arrived at the castle as soon as they heard about the taxes being paid. No easy feat either, since they were both wanted by the Dragon Board. When they arrived, there was work going on inside the place, as well as on the lawns. He'd always thought they had the most beautiful lawns, but of late, there hadn't been funds to care for it, mores the pity. Edwin supposed there might have been some money had they not been on trip after trip lately. They'd decided that traveling rather than feeling the pinch of the house in need of things was more practical. Well, not practical for most, but it had been a great deal of fun for them.

Then as they made their way to the front door, to claim it as their own again, the magic surrounding the place had nearly taken them to their knees. And entrance was impossible. He had to look that one up when neither one could enter.

The rules were very clear on that. Whoever made a home of a dragon their own, it belonged to them until such time an agreement could be made between them. Or death. He wasn't sure how they could make an agreement between them and their son—he'd never been one to give them what they wanted—so killing him would have to do. And now his mate, who would be able to hold the home from them as much as their son had. Hanson hadn't been all that nice for a great many years.

"We'll make him give us back our home. He had no right

36

to do that to us." Edwin figured that he had every right to claim the home as he had, but it had come as a surprise that he'd been able to. He asked his wife if she thought that they could make him. "Yes. He's our son, isn't he? He'll do as he's told or else."

"I don't think that's going to be a good threat, my dear. If he's strong enough to claim the home, then he's no longer going to have to listen to us. Like you said, he hasn't for a long time, but now he's a bit stronger, I guess. It's the way things go." He'd read that too, how a child of dragons could claim their family home if he was stronger than his sires and if he had good reason. He had both power and reasoning, it seemed. "But we're going to have to get something from him. A home, or even the cash to find us one. I do not care for living out in the open as we are. There is all kinds of trouble lurking about."

There really wasn't anything that could hurt them. They both had the magic to shelter themselves in a cave. And being what they were, nothing bothered them. Not even a fly or a worm. But it was galling, to say the least, that they were stuck like this. Like nothing more than commoners with nary a coin to their name.

It was true about dragon tears. They could and would, when necessary, form tears that would amount to a great deal of money. But that too had been something that had been taken from them when they'd been called to the Board. Until they went before them, served their sentence or paid their fine, they'd only be able to use the barest of magic. Shifting for sure, and protection, but little else.

"Should we contact him? Find out where he might be? I would like to go home again, see what sort of things he's having done for our home." Geraldine looked so hopeful,

37

he hated to tell her that it wouldn't work. "You'd think we beat him more than we did or something to be treated like this. I'm betting that if I was that English woman, he'd be breaking his.... That's where he is. With that upstart boy and his parents."

"Do you really think so? We could go there. We'd have to fly in the darkness so that we'd not be caught. To be honest with you, Geraldine, I wonder why the Board hasn't come here to see us as yet. He would have had them watching for us, don't you think?" She nodded and called him a little bastard. "Yes, well, he always has been. Jessie too. But we took care of that problem."

He'd hated to do what he'd done to his daughter. But she'd been so greedy about things. Like magic, and wanting to travel with Hanson. When they'd started draining her of her magic, she'd become worse than before. Whining about how she'd not felt good, that she was too weak to be moved. They'd had to leave her when they fled the area, and knew that she'd die. Not that either of them cared...Edwin and Geraldine hadn't even wanted children, and had two at once. Had it not been a matter of public record for their kind, they might well have destroyed them before they'd taken their first breaths.

"It's really a shame that we don't have Jessie here. She could have given us enough jewels to get us a good start on things. I guess we should have taken better care that she didn't die when we needed her most. Oh well, water under the bridge now, I suppose." He nodded; it was a shame. She'd been so useful up until the end. "Perhaps we can do the same to Hanson. Hold his mate, whatever she is, as prisoner until we get what we need from him."

"That's a right good plan, love. You are brilliant." She said that she knew that, but appreciated him saying so. "Hanson will do what he needs to keep her safe, don't you think?"

"Yes, I do. I surely do. We'll leave as soon as it's dark enough to hide us. Then we'll get there and make sure he knows that we're in charge of such things. And that mother of Danburn's, we'll make her pay us a fine while she's about. That way we can keep her in her place as well. Never cared for them, not at all." He told her that he would take care that she knew that as a lord, and her a lowly female, he demanded respect. Yes, Geraldine told him, he did. Especially from someone like her. "Look yonder, love."

The Board was at their home. Not that they could see them, who they were, but they knew the blue magic of their kind well enough. Hiding deeper in the caves, they waited, not making a sound until they were sure it was dark enough for them to leave. They'd know...the Board would know that they'd been there, he supposed. But there was no hope for it now. They'd be gone soon enough, and then they'd take care of their fines. Senseless, Edwin thought, to be fined for something as silly as not paying their dues when they came up. Then having to pay fines to take care of the fines. Stupid way to do business, he thought.

Every time they peeked to see if the Board was still there, they had to go back. It was as if they were waiting on them to make a move. Well, Edwin knew more tricks than they did, and they could wait them out. As dragons, deep within the cave they'd find food. As humans, they'd be able to hide in smaller caves.

But when the sun came up the next morning and the Board was still there, they decided they had waited them out long enough. They needed to get to their son and have him take care of whatever it was they wanted because as Edwin talked with his mate and only true love, they'd come to realize there was no reason for them to be hunting them.

"The fees have been paid or they'd have taken our home. Having it worked on, it means that it's cleared up. And since we know that the bank has been paid off as well, then we're in the clear. What on earth could they be wanting from us now? Our heads? Not likely. We're royalty. Besides, we've done nothing wrong so far as they know." Geraldine said he was right. "Of course I am. We'll not take any chances, however, and find us an opening at the other end and be on our way. Once we have Hanson, things will be ever so much better."

They left at dusk. It was hard flying in the darkness these days. They had to watch out for flying planes, as well as little things that were as bright as the sun at times. He thought they called them drones or something like that. Annoying little things that took pictures. It was forbidden, resulting in death to those that allowed pictures to be taken of themselves in dragon form.

So to avoid everything that they could, they flew in short flights and rested between each one. Edwin had a feeling that they were not in the best of shape from the way their rest periods were longer than their flying time. He also knew that their dragons weren't very happy with them either. For some reason, they were being stubborn about the smallest of things.

The first night was the worst they'd ever flown. Even when they were headed to their home, it hadn't been this bad. There were spies out everywhere. And they weren't being paranoid either…they saw them. Blue magic was everywhere they tried to land to rest.

"Why blue magic, do you suppose?" Geraldine asked him what he meant. "Why does the Board use blue to show off their magic? Isn't that sort of like telling us where they are? Seems like they'd use nothing, or even smoke-like magic, to hide the fact that they're about and waiting on someone."

"It's only blue to let others know that they're around, such as other dragons, so they know that someone is in trouble. My mother said that it was surrounding me all my life. I guess she might have been right. Anyway, it's there to warn others that they're around so perhaps they don't get in their way." She thought about it, and he waited for her answer. "Yes, I think you're right, it does seem to give the bad people a good indicator, but then I'm not in charge of such things."

Whoever was in charge, they were going to have to get up pretty early in the morning to catch them. Edwin was proud of the fact that not only had they gotten away from them, but they were making good time, he supposed, in going to get their son. Soon this would all be a nightmare best forgotten. And Edwin prided himself on forgetting things he didn't want to deal with.

~~~

Quinn sat on the deck, not looking up at the men flying around. Well, dragons flying around. There were dragon's flying in the sky just above her, and one of them was her mate. She looked over when the other chair made a scraping sound. Kendrick and Cassie had joined her.

"You all right?" Hiding her hand under her shirt, she nodded. Every time she'd looked at her hands, they were shaking like a leaf in a storm. They'd know, she guessed, but there wasn't any point in advertising it. "No, you're not. You're just about a breath away from freaking out. If you were to talk about it, I'm sure you'd feel better."

"No, I won't." She looked at Cassie when she laughed. "You don't find this the least bit wrong? I mean, I don't want to be a stick in the mud here, but I'm only human. And that's all I've ever been."

Kendrick laughed and started speaking. "So was I. I mean, when I met up with Danburn, he wasn't the least bit nice, nor very polite either. He was a prick and a stick in the mud. And Noah, the man that helps us run this house, he thought I wasn't good enough for his master. He has since changed his mind, and now thinks that Danburn isn't good enough for me." Quinn laughed. She could see the other gentleman thinking that. He worshiped Kendrick. "Yes, so you see, we don't really concern ourselves with social standing or anything like that."

"It's not a social standing, not really. I mean...he's special." Kendrick said that she was as well. "That remains to be seen. But I have to make sure that Carmine and I are cared for. That we have a home that is safe, a school that I can afford. All the things that I need to provide for her."

"I'm pretty sure that Hanson is in a better position to do that with you than most people you know." That was the point, she thought. He was better at everything that she wanted to do. This time when Kendrick spoke, it was softer... she could almost feel the warmth of her words. "You know when I told you that Rett was looking into things for you? Well, he's found you an attorney that has gone to the state about your case. They're settling out of court with you. If you agree on the amount that they're giving you, you'll have it in an account that we'll set up for you in twenty-four hours. Its six million dollars, and no cost to you with anything else that has been on the table. Such as insurance and an education for you and your sister should you want it."

A feeling of guild flooded through Quinn. "I don't need that." Kendrick said it was done, if she agreed with them. "But what about the others there? Mrs. Smith's family? The woman who shot us? What do they get?" Kendrick said they all got the same amount and the same benefits. "Why would he do that? I mean, I guess we could all use it. I could really set my sister up with a good college education without her having to work at all. And then there is housing. But it's so much."

"There's more things that you have to think about too," Cassie said softly to Quinn. "Other than the money and what it's going to do for you and your sister. Hanson's parents. And what they'll do or demand of Hanson. And I'm sure, from what I've heard, that they will." Cassie started pacing the deck as she continued. "I met them once. That was all it took to know that they're horrid people. But they've been stripped of everything that they held dear to their hearts."

"You mean their child, Jessie?" Cassie told her. "Money? How is that more important than a child dying? Or losing your home?"

"Because they're greedy people." She'd not realized that the men had stopped flying and were now on the ground, and she was startled when Hanson spoke to her. He sat down on the swing as he told her the rest. "My sister contacted me just before she died. We didn't have long…she was as close to death as she could be. She told me that they'd killed her, and that they were on the run. They left her there, alone in that house, while they ran away instead of taking care of their child. For that alone, they'll pay the price. As high of one that I can inflict on them. Then there is the house, and the people that were there depending on them. My parents will come here and try their best to get me to relent. And they'll do that by trying to harm you and Carmine. But they won't get near either of you. I promise you."

"Thank you, but I don't understand how anyone could

do that to their own. Why did they not help her, or at least call someone in that could?" He shrugged and moved over so that Kip and Dana could join him on the swing. "They're dragons too. I don't know why that just occurred to me, but they're going to be big dragons as well. And powerful."

"Not so much now. When they left without coming before the Board, they were stripped of most of their magic. They can shift if they wish, but it takes them longer to recover should they get hurt in either form. They can protect themselves too, and shelter each other. They, however, cannot make tears, and without that, no money." Quinn asked what that meant. "The story about dragons making tears that turned to jewels is true. That's how most of us, if not all, financed our lives through the lean years. Now...well, now it's not so easy to turn such items in for money. But we have them. We have stores of them, my dear. For anything you wish."

She decided to ignore his comment for now. Stores of gems? What did he think she was going to do with them? Buy out a store? Not her. She saved for a rainy day, which of late seemed to be a daily thing.

"So, they're coming here. To what? I'm assuming that since they're not well liked, there has to be a reason for them to come here. What is it?" He told her it was her and him, as mates. "There is no you and me. And how would they even know about me? I've barely gotten a handle on you being a dragon, much less being your mate."

"The moment I took your blood into my body, they knew. I didn't know that it would work that way or I would have spoken to you more about it. But since I'm who I am and they're who they are, they knew." She told him he was being confusing. "Yes, I'm trying very hard to give you this a little at a time."

44

"What he's so gallantly trying not to tell you is that he is a powerful being. Not as powerful as Danburn, but nearly so, making him the second most powerful dragon ever born." Dana stood up as he spoke. "We're going to leave this to you two. If you have any questions, my dear, you can ask us, and we'd be more than happy to answer them for you. But you need to listen to him. The McClains are coming, and when they get here, they're going to be pissed off and stupid. I say stupid because their anger is going to make them do dumb things, and you might well be hurt from it."

They all went in the house and she sat down on the chair as far from Hanson as she could get. Carmine was in the house, playing with some of the toys that had been bought for her, so she wasn't worried about her. But this man…he didn't scare her, but she was a little frightened about what he might tell her next.

"I could run away. I mean, they don't know who I am and I could just leave." He told her that wouldn't work. "Why not? I could go to another city or state. Hide out until they're taken care of."

"If you leave, then I'm going to go with you. You're a part of me now. Someone that I need to protect with my life. And that would include your sister. She's as much a part of my life as you are now." Quinn didn't like any of this. "Can you come over here? Sit next to me?"

She didn't move. Quinn wasn't sure why, but she thought if she moved to sit next to him, she'd not be able to clear her mind. There were questions going around and around in her head so quickly that it was hard for her to touch on a single one.

"I got some news today. Apparently, Rett had someone sue the state for money for us. I got six million dollars. I could buy us a house, my sister and me, and no one would ever know that we were here." He nodded. "You don't think that will work, do you?"

"No. I'm sorry, but it won't. Not only will I need to be with you, but your scent is all over this house and lawn. It would be easy to find you." She looked at him and he smiled at her. "You're very beautiful. Did you know that? And one of the kindest people I know. But my parents will destroy you, simply because of what you are to me."

"But I don't know what I am to you. Or why you want there to be anything between us. I'm not a dragon. I have a sister that I have to put first in my life. I have money now, but I don't have a clue how to be rich like you guys. If someone were to ask me what sort of clothing I like to wear, my answer would be cheap. On sale." He smiled gently at her. "You have a pair of jeans on that cost more than I make in a day at one of my jobs. Boots that are worth nearly what I make in a week. You're all put together, and I'm a mess."

"Okay, first...I have no idea what you mean by not knowing how to be rich. You just be yourself, and that's all I want. Clothing? I love what you have on now. But if you were naked, under me, I'd like that better." Her face got hot. "You could have expensive boots should you want them. And I buy on sale as well. Just because I have money, it doesn't mean that I spend it unwisely. And in answer to your question about why I want something between us? Because you are my life. My heart and soul. You will complete me in ways that I cannot imagine now. I will be happy, happier than I've ever been because you are beside me. And your sister? She'll be my daughter, or my sister too if you wish it."

When he stood up and came to her, she watched him. Suddenly she was up and then sitting down on his lap. When she started to struggle he held her still, and she could feel his erection beneath her. Sitting as still as she could, Quinn looked into his eyes.

"I can see him." He didn't move but held her there. "Your dragon. I mean, I saw him when you shifted earlier, but now, it's like he's posing for me."

"He's there for you. When I was younger, a great deal younger, he would speak to me. It wasn't until I spoke with my sister that I realized that he was a part of me, but also someone else. Like he was his own person." Quinn nodded. "The reason I tell you that is because he spoke to me about you. And what he thinks of you."

"I'm sure that it's not all that flattering." He told her it was. "What did he say? That I was a fool? That I'm only a buffoon and have no business being around you?"

"Nay, he said that you are the most gorgeous woman he's ever seen. That you were his mate and that he was happy for it." He pulled her closer to him, his mouth just a breath away from hers. And when he brushed it over hers, she moaned slightly. "Let me kiss you, Quinn. Please?"

Nodding, afraid that she'd disappoint him on so many levels, she moaned again, this time louder, and turned in his arms. It was then that she realized she wanted him, as much as she thought he did her.

The kiss that he'd given her had turned into so much more than she had thought. His mouth was hot, like his skin was. His breath was marking her, burning in her in ways that she had never thought to enjoy.

"More. I need more."

She felt like she needed it as well. All of him. And when she was lifted and set away from him, she thought he'd changed his mind. It wasn't until he shifted again and they were soaring through the sky that she knew he was taking her someplace private.

Chapter 4

He knew that he had to take it easy. The need that he had for her, for his mate, was powerful. Getting them to the trees atop the mountain was the best plan he could think of in making her his. Hanson had seen it when they were flying around, and thought it a very private and beautiful place. The most perfect place he could think of for making her his forever. Setting her down on the ground, he stepped back from her again and started to shift.

"Wait. I want to see you again." He nodded but didn't move. He was afraid of her seeing him this way, up close, but he'd do anything for her. As she moved around him, careful of his tail, he laid down when she asked him to. "When we were together down there, all I could think about was how you could smash me with just a single flick of your tail. But now, I can see that not only are you handsome, but you're very well built too. That sounded better in my head."

It's all right. I understand. I'm built for my safety, and yours now. The scales on my underbelly are thicker and have a bit more magic on them to keep my heart from being pierced. Also, there are

49

spikes along my back that stick up when I'm in a fight. She asked if she could see them. *Sure. But I'll do it for a trade. You show me something of yours.*

"I do believe you've seen more of me than I thought you should have by now." He laughed. She was absolutely delightful. "Yes, all right. But I get to choose what I show you. All right?"

He said yes. If she didn't move fast enough for him and his dragon, he'd just take things off her. So when she asked to see his head gear or whatever it was called, he told her that it was called his helmet, the top of his head's armor, then he lay down on the ground so she could see it better.

"Holy shit." He had to laugh. It was funny how he'd not realized it would be so much fun to show her how he was when in fighting mode. "It's like you have a helmet, just like you said, on the top of your head. And it's harder than your other armor. I'm not saying you have a hard head, but you really do. And horns. I suppose you can use them to gouge your enemy, right?"

Yes, you're right. I have the same things on my legs too. Your turn. Take something off. She pointed out that she would only show him something, not take off her clothing. *That's not fair. I want to see some of that lovely skin. And see those breasts that have been tantalizing me for days now. I wonder, are your nipples always so pink, or did I do that to them?*

Quinn took off her sweater and let her blouse open. He'd already seen those lovely nipples when they'd been in the house, and was looking forward to tasting a great deal more of her. And when she pulled her boots off, he had a glimpse of what she'd been talking about when she'd spoken of his boots. Hers were full of holes and worn through in a great many places. He spied tape on them, he was sure to hold them together. Hanson was going to take care of that first thing.

"Now I'd like to see those leg armors, please." He told her what they were called. "Whatever. Don't tease me. Just wondering, do all dragons look like you do when in battle mode? Or are you prettier than each other? Do you primp around, looking in the ocean to see how you look before you try and kill someone?"

He snorted a small flame toward her, and watched as she leaned over it to warm her hands. He'd forgotten that she might be cold with their play, and made the flame a little bigger when she stepped back.

We're all prettier than each other…I thought you'd know that. She nodded. *Take off something else. If you do, I'll make it worth your while.*

"I think you just want me to be naked." He said that he did. "Why? I mean, isn't it true that if you've seen one naked woman then you've seen them all?"

Perhaps to some men. But what you don't understand is that you're my *naked woman.* She nodded and he felt his heart beat faster. *I'm going to shift, then I'm going to strip you down to see you. Or you can do it for me and save on you having something to wear when we head back to the house. And so you know, I'm going to take you shopping tomorrow, you and Carmine, and have some fun. Wait, the day after tomorrow. We'll do some Christmas shopping too. It'll be Black Friday, lots of sales and people.*

When she unbuttoned her pants, he let his dragon go. It was harder than he thought it would be…his dragon wanted to see her as well. But for now, he was allowing him his mate, and Hanson could not wait.

"I've done this before. The sex thing?" He nearly laughed, but caught himself just in time. "I'm not saying that I'm terrible at it, but no one has ever come back for seconds. It's sort of…I guess blah. You know, sort of uneventful. I suppose men can get off with anything, but for me, it's not all that special. Nor, I guess, for them, because they took off like I'd shot them from a gun."

"Really? Perhaps you've not been with the right partner. Or they sucked at it." She smiled at him, and he could have lived with that picture in his mind for the rest of his life. "You really are beautiful. And I'm going to show you just how much you mean to me."

"You don't have to say those sorts of things to me, Hanson. I know what I look like." He pulled her now naked body to his and had her look at him. "I'm afraid."

"Of me?" She shook her head and told him she was afraid of disappointing him. "Never. Not even if you were to just let me have my way with you, you'd never disappoint me. However, I plan to make you the most sated woman on earth, as well as mine. Do you know what that means?"

"Yes. You will mark me." He said that he'd done that, he was talking about her taking his blood as well. "I can do that. I…I think I'd really enjoy that as well."

He didn't want to rush her, but all he could think about was having her taste his blood. When he cut his throat for her, a small wound that he wasn't worried about, she laid her mouth over it before he could tell her to. It was like having a furnace put to his skin, but in a good way. And when she drew at the wound, then swallowed, his cock stretched hard and he pulled her toward him.

"I need you." He nodded when she lifted her head from him. "Please. I need to feel you inside of me."

He took her to the tree that was closest to them. Once there, he picked her up and slid into her. It was as easy as that. But not as normal as it sounded. Anything with her, even a touch, was all new to him. Like the first breath he took, the first time his heart beat, it was with her, each new thing, and it made it better.

She was so wet, her body so ready for his, that he didn't pause in his need to make her his. When he thought he could move without coming right then, he kissed her hungrily and then pressed his forehead to hers.

"I'm going to tell you something. I know you're not used to us, paranormals and all, but we love hard and forever. I love you, Quinn." She closed her eyes and he asked her to look at him. "I love you. And I will be here for you for the rest of our days. And when you love me, if you ever can, I will be the happiest man alive."

"I don't know what to do." He moaned when she moved. "You feel good there, inside of me. Do you suppose, I don't know, you could move a little?"

He did as she asked and watched her face. "Do you like that?" She nodded and told him more. "Are you going to be greedy every time we have sex?"

"If you need step by step instructions, then yes, I'm going to be very greedy. Oh, Christ yes." He didn't take her hard, as much as he wanted to do that, but he did move in and out of her slowly. "More, Hanson, please, I need so much more."

He took her harder, trying his best to give her as much pleasure as he could before he took his own. And when she came, screaming out not just his name but telling him no more, he pulled her from the tree and took her to the ground. It was there that he gave her all that he had.

She came several times before she pulled his throat to her mouth again. This time when she put her mouth over the wound and drew deeply, he cried out as well. His cock didn't just release, but seemed to detonate inside of her several times before he dropped atop her, exhausted. Her small giggle made him look down at her.

"I think you broke me." He grinned at her. "I feel like I've been given the greatest gift of all time, and the best sex too. You're amazing." He told her it was all her. "I don't think so. Had I been even half as good as that, then I'd be having men lined up out the street for a toss in the hay."

"I'm a very jealous type; you should know that right now." She giggled again and moved her feet up and down his legs as he continued. Rolling to his back, he took her with him as she laid over him. "As I was saying, I'm a very jealous person. I wasn't before you, but right now I could easily get up and shift, then burn down the houses of every other male that has ever been in your life. And not think a thing about it."

"Men have never meant that much to me. I mean, they're fun for the most part, but they wanted so much more than I had to give them. Then my mom got ill, and there was my sister that needed me. There wasn't much time to date, much less get laid with all that going on." He told her he was sorry. "I'm not. Not really. I got to spend a few months with my mom and sister. Carmine is a good little girl, and doesn't get on peoples' nerves like some kids do. After Dad died, before my mom got sick, it was just the three of us. I had to work a lot, a great deal, but I'd do it all again for them."

"I know you would. I think that's what made me fall in love with you the first time I saw you." She moved so that her head was on his chest, and he held her. It was getting colder with night coming on, so he let a little of his dragon warm her up. "You should know a couple of things before my parents get here. First, you're an immortal. And since they've been stripped of their magic, they can't harm you in any way other than to remove your head."

"Well, color me shocked, but that is a biggie, don't you think?" He laughed. "I mean, will that be something I should worry about? Them coming up to me with swords drawn?"

"Yes." She stared at him then, and then laid back down. "They hate me. And I suppose with good reason. I've never been the type of child they wanted. My sister either. Not that it was my fault, not either of us. But they never wanted us, and didn't have any problems letting us know that. Daily. And when I left, the burden of being with them fell to my sister. But I could never get her to leave there. She, I think, felt that she might be able to change them, or to make them love us."

"And what sort of son did they want? One that is a gadabout? One that doesn't care for others as much as you do? I don't know what they could have wanted, but I think you're perfect." She looked at him again. "What is it they wanted you to do? I'm assuming that it wasn't legal, by any standards."

"I'm powerful. As you've been told, I'm the second most powerful dragon ever born, and I don't think they ever realized that. Or perhaps didn't believe it. And while that is one thing that neither one could control, there is also the added fact that I can control water and fire. Danburn is able to do that as well, in addition to the earth and the air. But, being their son, they thought that I should do what they wanted with my power." She nodded and told him to go on. "They are greedy, my parents. More so than most humans that I've come across in my lifetime. They thought that if I were to burn down some buildings that I owned in the town, then we could share in the insurance money. Or, if the bank were to say, catch fire by me, I could make sure that the money wasn't burned so that we could collect and share it as well. And in the event that you didn't catch this, their idea of sharing meant that I'd take the blame and them the profits. It's been that way for as long as I remember."

"That's so wrong. I mean, not even counting how illegal that is, what about the people that worked in those buildings? They'd be out of a job. And then there is the whole trickle-down theory...if they don't have a job, they're not spending money in the town, which means that they close up and more people are out of.... Didn't they think of those things?" She looked fiery mad, and he loved it. As long as her temper wasn't aimed at him, that was. Smiling at her when she laid her head back on his chest, he answered her question.

"Not as quickly as you have. And not without me pointing it out." He smiled, and then kissed her again. "I knew from the start that you were brilliant. My parents aren't going to realize what hit them with you in my corner."

"I'm not going to let them hurt you either. Just so you know, there won't be any illegal dealing while I'm around either. I need a book." He said that he could get her one. "Good. I'd like to know the rules before they get here. And I want to know them well. The Board, or whatever they're called, won't have a thing on me when I'm finished with these people."

He teased her while they dressed. She was cold, he could see that, but she never complained. Hanson warmed her up several times, but he'd get distracted when he touched her. Finally she told him to back off and leave her alone or they'd never get home. That was fine by him. He knew that their bedroom would be warmed up too.

Hanson took her back to the house as his dragon, and then told her he'd be back. He had a couple of things he had to do before tomorrow, and one of them was to find them a good home. He decided that he wanted to live near Danburn and the rest of the family. It might come in handy to have them all around. Plus, he wanted some privacy. Hanson wanted to hear her scream his name a lot more.

~~~

Geraldine wasn't happy about where they were staying. First of all, the hotel in town was full, and they wouldn't turn someone out for them. She explained to the proprietor several times who they were, but he only turned his nose up at her and waited on the next human that came in the door.

"I don't know what this world is coming to, Edwin, when a respectable dragon comes in and they act as if they're nothing." He pointed out that they more than likely didn't know they were dragons. "Yes, there is that. And I guess that's a good thing too. Once we figure out how to contact Hanson, then we'll come back here and make them do what we want. Have you been able to figure out where they are yet?"

"No. I know this is the area that the magic came from, but where they are I'm not so sure. It's as if they disappeared right after that happened." He sat down on the bench across from the hotel. "I guess we'll be staying in a cave a few more nights. We can't find us a place to stay, and even buying one is out of the question without funds. Damn it all to hell, Geraldine. We deserve better than this from these people. I'm betting that if our last name was English, we'd have the entire hotel and they'd be serving us on golden platters. I really hate those people."

"I know, but what can you do? Once we have Hanson doing things for us, and he will this time, then we'll be better off. All he needs to do is make sure that we can get in our home, and tell the Board to back off. I know that he's not the one that called them on us, but it sure would be nice to have our home back." She looked around the town and wondered why her son would even be here. "You think that Elissa is hanging around still? Or is she off on one of those trips again, you think? That woman traveled more than anyone I ever knew."

"Yes, and you were jealous of her every time you heard about it." She was, too, and smiled at her husband. "I guess we could have taken better care of our funds, and we could have gone on trips as well. What fun would that have been? Traveling all over the world and seeing such sights? I guess we could have traveled by dragon magic, but I've read up on those trips and they sure do treat you nice. Food forever flowing, entertainment out the wazoo. Also, there are things to do, like cards and such. I wish we could have gone on at least one of them, don't you think?"

"I do. And perhaps when we get this thing all settled up with the Board, we'll make arrangements to go on one. We have nothing tying us here anymore, not since Jessie finally died. What a burden she was to us. But she gave us magic when we needed it." He told her she had at that, and she wasn't any fun either. "All right, let's find us a place to lay our heads, and then in the morning, we'll find Hanson and this girl. I tell you, Edwin, I'm not going to stand for him being rude to us. He'll do as we tell him or he'll have to be short a mate. What he wants with one this late in his life is beyond me."

He'd thought of that as well, and he wondered what sort of being she was. There weren't that many dragons around anymore, none that he'd seen anyway, so he'd be mating beneath himself and his station in the world. But the thought of him mating at all worried him a little. A mate meant that he'd come into more of his magic, and he already had a great deal more than they did. What would this mean to them and getting him to do right by them? And another thing he worried about was, had Jessie contacted her brother before she died? If she had, then he would know that they'd killed her. That would not go over well with him or the Board. But, as his wife was so fond of saying, it was water under the bridge now.

"What are you thinking about? You seem so lost to me." He told her what he'd been thinking about for the last few days. "You think she's not a dragon? Well that would be just like him. Finding his mate and not even having the decency to find himself a dragon."

"I don't think he had a choice." He hadn't, but that didn't stop Geraldine from complaining about his choices like he had one. "I don't know what I'm to think about any of this. I mean, Jessie could have told him all sorts of things before she died. You know as well as I that they were very close. Sickening, I think, the way they loved each other. We should have finished her off before we left, don't you think?"

"Well, it's all water under the bridge now, don't you think?"

He nodded as they made their way out of the town to the mountains. He was ready to enter one of the larger openings when he felt the magic. It was powerful, and he had a sense of danger too. "Edwin? What is that?"

Her voice was low, as if she were afraid that whoever had put the magic here would hear them. Edwin was afraid as well. Not of anyone hearing him, but that a being so powerful as to shield a mountain from them would have untold powers. He was both relieved and afraid that it wasn't Hanson.

"I don't know. I mean, I'm not even sure that I want to know who might have been able to do this." She nodded and moved closer to him. He thought of shifting again to see if he could enter as a dragon, but was afraid of that as well. It was as if someone had known they were going to be there. He said as much to his mate.

"I hope not. I don't know…. Edwin, it's not that English boy is it? I mean, he does live around here, doesn't he? Could it be him?" He knew in that moment that it was him. When he told her what he thought, she shivered. "Perhaps we can just forget this whole thing and return to our home. It might be finished by now, and the magic lifted for us to enter."

"You know as well as I that it is not. And if we do not have Hanson take care of this thing with the Board, then we'll have them at our tails too. And as much as it pains me to say this, we need him." She shivered again. "Let's just shift, lay out here in the trees, and get some rest. Whoever is doing this, no matter what reason they have for doing so, we'll take care of it in the morn. And perhaps whatever it is might be gone by then too." He hoped so, anyway.

They found themselves a spot as close to the mountain as they dared go. The trees were losing their leaves, so it had been easy to gather enough for them to have a soft bed. Of course, they couldn't burn a fire—that part of their magic had been taken from them—but they did find some meat…a scrawny deer that was barely enough for one of them, much less both.

As they finished their meal, they curled around each other and lay down. But Edwin couldn't sleep. Something or someone was out there, and he was afraid of them.

When they'd been ready to birth their hatchlings, they'd had a plan. They'd be crushed under the weight of a rock slide, or there would be an intruder that crushed them. Either way, they were not going to have the children come into the world to ruin their lives. But the Board had come upon them when they were being brought into the world, and as they watched over the eggs, they also made note of their conditions. Such as there was no way for an intruder to find them, and the walls were safe and secure. They had even put a little of their own magic around the children so that they'd be safer. Mores the pity.

So, with a great deal of fanfare, the children came into the world healthy and for the most part, happy. But neither of the parents were. A burden such as those hatchlings were hadn't done much for them. Not until much later, when they came into their own magic. Then things took a nice turn. But that, too, didn't last long. They never wanted to help their parents as much as Edwin thought they should have.

Even as the years went by, the two of them, Jessie and Hanson, seemed to have the best of luck. Not in their opinion, but that of the world. Neither of them had wanted children… not anything at all to do with them. But they grew to be adults without much help from either him or Geraldine. Then Hanson left his sister at home, with the promise of returning for her when she was better. It was a promise that he wasn't able to make good on, they'd seen to that.

They had poisoned her. He wasn't ashamed that they had. It was necessary to get her to do what they wanted. When she was weak, as she had been, it had been a piece of cake to drain her of her magic and use it. Also, her tears had been very beneficial. When she was ill the tears were shed in pain, and he and Geraldine had collected them daily. Now, looking back on it, they probably should have stored a few of them away for their escape. As it was, they'd left without nary a coin to their name, nor even a bit of anything from the house. Not that there was much there anyway, after they'd sold most of it for their fun.

61

The house had been another dragon's. Right now he couldn't think of his name or why he'd been able to take it from him, but they had, and had lived in the castle for a great many years. Even the furniture and statues had been left behind. They'd sold off what they could for the coin to buy another pretty that had caught their eye. What he wouldn't give to go back to the house, take some of the items that had been too large for them to move, and destroy them. Just so Hanson couldn't have them.

He slept fitfully all night. And when the sun came up over the mountain, he was glad for the light. Sitting up, he shifted back to his counterpart and foraged in the woods for things to eat. He thought about taking some back to Geraldine, but decided that she could get her own. Besides, he was starving, and he thought of this as being somewhat her fault. She had gotten with child for them. When he returned to where he'd left her, she was still resting. Leaving her there, he made his way up to the mouth of the cave again to look around.

Edwin knew that a dragon had done this. He wasn't sure it was meant for him and his mate, but to keep all manner of creatures out. To his way of thinking there had to be something of value in the cave, because why else would you guard it like that? But no matter what he tried, he could not enter the place to check it out.

Frustrated, he went back to Geraldine and sat on a rock until she woke. When she took too long in that, he began to pick up stones and toss them at her head. It was funny really, but having fun at her expense was going to cost him. And as soon as she woke, she attacked him and knocked him back onto a stone, and he hit his head.

"Why must you be so stupid?" He woke, his head bleeding down his cheek as she sat there in front of him complaining.

"Time and time again, I have told you that I'm not easy to wake. And being out here, in all this wilderness with that cave up there…well, you're very lucky that I only cracked your head and didn't burn you."

"I was only playing." She huffed at him. "You've been sleeping forever, and I was bored. I was playing around, hoping to wake you so that we might get this done. Now look. I've a wound on my head that won't heal right away, and you've soiled my shirt too. I'll have to use a bit of the magic to make me presentable."

When he was as good as he could get with the restrictions on them, he glared at her a little more before he finally smiled. He could never stay mad at her for very long. She was his life and his love. Nothing would ever come between them, not again. As soon as they made their way back down the mountain, he knew a new kind of fear. His son was with his friend, the English boy, and he didn't think things could get any worse. Then he spotted her. Elissa English was as regal and as bitchy as he remembered her to be. And his son was with her.

Chapter 5

Hanson saw them standing across the street from him. His parents were indeed in the area, and they looked worse than he'd ever seen them. He had thought about going over to them, introducing them to his mate and Danburn, but decided that he would let them come to him. Besides, he didn't want Quinn or Carmine hurt. Kendrick and Elissa could and would take care of themselves.

Danburn had told Hanson that the earth had told him they had spent a bad night in the woods, and he was glad for it. So was Hanson. As they came closer to them, he told Quinn and Carmine to stay behind him. Carmine did it without hesitation, but Quinn stood by his side. He was afraid for her, and proud of her too.

"Hanson. What are you doing here? Did you know that we've been closed up from our home? You need to fix that." His father didn't even bother speaking to Danburn or his mom, which he supposed was stupid on his part as Danburn was his lord. "Come along now, and we'll get this taken care of before something befalls us. And the Board is looking for

65

us. You should have told them you'd pay the fines for us. It's your duty as our son."

"I hope something else does befall you. It's what you deserve. And it's past the point of paying fines for your misdeeds. You have to face them to get your sentencing." He looked at Quinn when she spoke. "You have no right coming here and expecting him to bail you out of trouble when you've gotten yourself into it all on your own. You know the rules, don't you? How you have to abide by them to the letter? If you haven't, then perhaps you should take a long look at them, as I did. And now, here you are making trouble with the humans. Are you so stupid that you can't make sure you stay out of more trouble? Or is it what you want? I think it's that...you like being the center of attention, even if it is in trouble."

"Who are you to dare speak to me in such a way? Hanson, you'll teach your woman to know her place when we're here. I see you're still keeping company with the upstarts too." His dad looked at Danburn and Kendrick, and then looked back at him. "Did I not tell you that he'd be a bad influence on you? And now look. We're out of our home, and you're acting like you have not a care in the world. We need you to talk to the Board on our behalf."

"No." He started to turn away from them, keeping an eye on Carmine as he did so. "Come along, honey, we'll get you some new boots while we're at it as well."

"You will not turn your back on me."

Hanson wasn't sure what happened, but turned back to his dad when he heard a shriek, only to find him down on the ground with his arms up behind his back. And he was screaming to be let go, yet there was no one around him. It wasn't until he looked at Carmine that he understood what was going on.

"Let me go this minute, Hanson, or so help me I'll fire you up until you cannot walk again."

Ignoring him for a moment, he got down on his knees and looked at Carmine. She was concentrating hard on what she was doing, and that made him a little nervous. Saying her name, she glanced at him and his father was released. It was obvious that his wrist was broken, and it looked like he might have strained his back too. But as soon as he was able to stand, his parents took off running in the other direction, his father limping like he was hurt a great deal.

"Are you all right?" She nodded, and then wrapped her arms around his neck and held him. Standing, he guided them all into the mall and away from his parents. Before he got too far Danburn stopped him, but Hanson wasn't sure he could talk about it now, and he needed answers first. *Not here. Okay? I'm not sure what is going on, but not here. Let's get some shopping done, then we can talk later. And I need to think. All right?*

She did that. It wasn't a question, but he told him yes anyway. *All right, but do you think that anyone knew she could?*

No, I don't.

They entered the first store they could and started looking for something to distract from what had just happened. He watched the little girl after she allowed him to put her down, and knew as surely as he was standing there that even Quinn didn't realize what her sister could do. Or if she did know, she might not have known how much she could do.

They bought her clothing at the next shop, mostly winter things that she could wear to school, as well as some fun things too. Lunch was a family affair, and Carmine seemed to be much more relaxed again, her old self. After a couple of more shops, they were going to go to the house he'd bought.

He felt badly for not bringing Quinn along when he'd gotten it, but felt the house couldn't have been more perfect for them if they'd ordered it. As they began filling a cart in the next shop, he wondered if Quinn had any hidden talent as well. It bore looking into.

They loaded the trunks of all the cars they'd brought, as well as arranged to have things delivered. Then they were all going to go to the new house to have a look around, but Carmine was getting cranky because she was so tired, and Danburn said he'd take her to his house for the night. Elissa fussed over her a bit, and then ended up buying the little girl books to read to her, as well as a few little things for her to call her own. When they left them, he looked at Quinn.

"Something happened." He nodded. "With your dad and mom. Can you tell me what it was? And how, while no one was touching them, he ended up with a broken wrist?"

"I think your sister.... No, that's not right. I know your sister did it. She has some magic within her that seems to be untapped." She asked him what he meant. "She knew how to use the magic to do what she wanted, but because she is so unsure of it, like the strength of it, she had to concentrate very hard not to tear his arm off, I believe. It's.... When she let him go, I could feel it, her strength, and how it didn't tire her like I would have thought it would."

"She isn't magical. How do you know that it wasn't Kendrick, or even Elissa? Danburn could even have done it." He shook his head as they headed to his car. "I don't believe you. She's just a little girl. And I've never seen her—"

When she stopped moving and stood there, he knew that she was remembering something. It had happened, and she hadn't counted it as real or she had brushed it off for some reason. Either way, it was something he thought he needed to know.

"What? You recalled something." She nodded. "Tell me, because as much as I'd like to keep my parents in the dark about her, I'm pretty sure once they think about it, they'll know it was her. And when they do, they'll take her to control her magic."

"When we were living at home, a few weeks before I got hurt, Carmine was keeping an eye on Mom while I ran to the store. When I returned…. I always thought that I'd been exhausted or something, but when I got back, I could have sworn that a glass was floating toward my mom. Could she do that too?"

"I don't know what sort of things she can do, but she did put my dad in an arm lock without any trouble. She could more than likely do a great many things, but hasn't told anyone for fear of being in trouble. We have to talk to her." She nodded. "But until then, we have a house to look over and make ours. There is even a pool in the back for Carmine, as well as it's within walking distance of Rett and Cassie's, for when the weather gets warm again."

The house was being worked on when they pulled in the drive. He'd wanted it painted, and then cleaned from top to bottom. Also, he'd taken it upon himself to have a suite of rooms set up for Carmine…her own bathroom, a small office for homework, as well as a little girl's room that any child would envy. He'd taken a peek into her mind to see just what she wanted.

It wasn't girly like he'd thought it would be. Not a speck of pink for this girl. Earth tones were there, greens, browns, blues, and dark oranges. Plants too, painted on the walls, as well as in planters all around the room. And her bathroom was decorated with frogs and fish, like a haven in a rainforest. Hanson couldn't have been happier at the way it was shaping up for the little girl. She had stolen his heart as much as Quinn had.

There were also enough bedrooms for them to have people over should they wish. The large yard was still being worked on when the house had come on the market, but had gone by the wayside when things were going bad for the contractors. That was why he'd gotten such a good deal on it...it was yet unfinished. He was excited to see what he could do with it, and was glad that Quinn seemed just as happy with it. He took her into the kitchen.

"I could cook in here, and have fun at it." He asked her if she enjoyed it. "Oh yes. I love cooking and baking. It was my dream when I was younger to have my own diner. But I have since realized that it's not a dream I could make happen."

"Why not? If you want to, anything is possible." She smiled at him, and he had a feeling she was humoring him. "I think you should go for it."

"I really can't. I mean, the sort of food that I'd cook, it's not what people go out wanting to eat. I'm more of a down home kind of cook. You know, fried chicken, green beans, homemade corn bread. Not the usual fare." He told her that sounded good. "Yes, for meals at home, not out."

He was going to look into that. Hanson thought it would be a good choice of restaurant fare, and decided that if anyone could do it, it would be her. And he'd be right there with her if she wanted. Smiling, he showed her the rest of the house, and they ended up in the master suite.

"I've ordered us a bed, a big one that we can have fun on. It'll be here in a couple of days." She wandered around the room and paused in front of the large picture window that looked out over Danburn's mountain and the lake beyond. "Anything you wish to change, it's all right with me. And if you don't like this house, we can keep looking and put it back on the market."

"Did you pay cash for this place?" He wondered at the question, but answered that he had. "And anything that we want, my sister and I, you'll provide that as well, using cash."

"Yes. I have a great deal of money, Quinn. We both do, even if you never touch the money that came to you from the settlement from the state. I want you to have the best." She turned and looked at him. "What's the matter, love? Have I upset you by doing this without you?"

"No, the house is perfect. I love it. But I've been thinking about what we're costing you, my sister and me." He told her that he loved her. "I know, but…how do you know you love me? How do you know that I'm your mate? Or for that matter, how did you know that this house would be perfect for us?"

"First of all, I do love you. I feel it deep inside my heart. I can't think without you there, I can't breathe without smelling a part of you on myself. I love you for no other reason than you are perfect for me. How do I know you're my mate? That's a little easier to explain." He moved toward her and asked her to trust him. "I want you to think of something. Something that I don't know about, nor have you told anyone else. All right?"

She said that she had it. And when he reached into her mind to tell her what she was thinking, he stumbled back a little and she smiled at him. It was right there for him to see.

"You love me?" She nodded. "Then why are you asking me about this? I love you more than anything."

"I wanted you to be sure. And I read that book, remember?

It said that only mates are able to read each other's minds, as well as any children of them. I'm assuming that since you knew what sort of boots and coat that Carmine wanted before I could have guessed, you think of her as your child too?" He nodded, smiling at her. "We're a package deal…you're aware of that, I know. But there is my mom's will that has to be read, and while I know that I have full custody of Carmine, I need to know what else Mom has set up. My mom had insurance… not much, but enough to cover a local college should Carmine want to go. But with this money from the state, I want her to be in a good enough position to go to anyplace she wants, and not have to worry about working."

"I think that's a wonderful idea. But I must tell you, today when she wrapped her arms around me, it was like having sunshine spread over my wings on a beautiful summer day." Quinn told him that was the way it made her feel too. "And this power that she has, it'll mean nothing more than she'll need to be watched over more carefully so that no one takes her for their own use."

"Like your parents." He said that was right. "If they come near her, there will be hell to pay. I might only be human, but I'm telling you right now, Hanson, they'll regret touching her with every fiber of their body, as well as anything else I can think of."

"That's my girl."

The rest of the house was just as lovely as he'd hoped. And not only did she like it as much as he did, she also suggested a few things that he'd not thought of. Like the sunporch on the back being screened in, as well as a garden for the faeries around. He thought she might have been teasing, but he'd have to show her that they really were around them.

~~~

72

Danburn wasn't going to sit around and wait for the McClains to make trouble. His contact at the Board was coming to see him in an hour, and he had all the information he needed to have them taken in. As soon as the earth had relayed the information to him, he had made the call. Kendrick came into the room just as he was putting the phone back in the cradle.

"Did you know that your mom kept all your baby things?" He said that he sort of knew that. "Well, here's a good one for you. Your baby things are worth more as antiques than what it would cost us to put in a whole wing for the baby."

"Mom told me that everything was outdated and couldn't be used. Are you planning to sell them?" She told him no, she was just making small talk. "Ah. Anything I need to know about? You don't usually care for small talk."

"I went to the doctor today. This morning." He asked her why she'd not taken him with her. "Because I had some questions to ask him, and you get all huffy when he doesn't answer things to your expectations."

"I do not get huffy." She just cocked her pretty brow at him. "All right, I get a little huffy, but I wouldn't have to if he wasn't so long winded. Why does he not just answer the question without going around the bend several times before he comes back to it?"

"Because, mister smarty-pants, some people—most people—haven't been around forever and know it all. Not to mention, you terrify the man." He told her she was exaggerating. "I most certainly am not. When he found out that you weren't with me, he actually laughed a little, then seemed to relax. It was like I'd lifted a large albatross from him."

"I am not an albatross." Again she looked at him oddly,

but this time like he was missing the point. "I only growled at him that one time when he wanted you to take off your shirt so he could do that test on you. How was I supposed to know that he does that all the time?"

"You know what I have to do? I ask questions before I go all nut-job on people when they're trying to help someone." He growled low. "I heard that, don't think I didn't."

"What did he say to you?" He was being childish, but since she was enjoying herself, he continued. "And he'd better not have touched you in any way that would mean I have to go there and burn his offices down."

"You're impossible. But he did tell me that I'm doing well and that things are going right on time. The due date is the same for me, July second, and we can expect a nice sized baby, he said, because your mom told me how much you weighed." She grinned at him. "Of course, he knew who you are and what you are, so that helped him remember that she would be a big baby because of that. He wasn't even shocked when I told him you weighed thirty-six pounds."

"Yes, well, Mom said that being as large as I was, it made me healthier than most of the babies born at that time." He asked her to come sit on his lap and she said no. "Why not? I have a need for you."

"You always have some sort of need that has me naked. I have to go and meet Cassie and Quinn at the school, then we're having lunch. Under the circumstances, I thought it a good idea that we put Carmine in the local pack school, where she can be protected and her magic wouldn't cause a problem."

"I'm supposed to have a talk with Hanson today too. He said that he was going to find out what he could from the little girl, but he wasn't betting on too much. I think she's had this from birth but no one noticed it." He leaned back in his chair and thought about what she'd done. "What do you suppose she is? I mean, as far as any of us know, Quinn is human and so was her mom. But this, this is really strange, don't you think?"

"No. I've read about things like this before. Basically everyone has the ability to control things with their mind, but few actually develop it. Perhaps she knew it early on and it was working for her, so she kept working at it." He asked her in what way. "I don't know. Maybe she figured out that she could get her a bottle when she wanted it. Or that she could bring a favorite toy or something to her. When that worked, she decided that she could do more and practiced."

He could see that, he supposed, but he'd hopefully know more when he spoke to Hanson. Also, he had some more information on his parents. As he began working on the things from his businesses, he thought vaguely of the McClains. They were in for some big trouble with the Board, and he was going to make sure that they were punished to the fullest extent of their laws. Also, they'd not reported to him that they were around, and that would get them into trouble with him too. Being a dragon king had some perks, he thought.

The rest of the afternoon wore on, and he was surprised by what time it was when he heard the doorbell. Going to the front of his home, he was surprised and pleased to see two of the Board members with Hanson. None of them looked to be upset, and he invited them in. He had a feeling that things were about to come to a head with Hanson's family.

"They're still in your woods…we've been there to have a look around. Also, you should know that they've taken some of your deer as food. Nasty business, this. I suppose that we should have expected it." Danburn said that he was aware of that, but didn't have any problem with them being fed. "Yes, well, you might rethink that when you see the carnage they have left there. At least three dozen dead deer, as well as a den of raccoons that have been killed and left. Not even making a meal of them."

Danburn told them he'd take care of it. "I'll go and see them today and talk to them. When is it you're going to go?" They looked at Hanson, then back at him. "What's happened?"

"I'm a member of the Board now." Danburn laughed, then congratulated him. "Yeah, well, I get to exact my own kind of law on them for things that they've done. It should be a blast, don't you think?"

"I'm sure that you'll be fair and reasonable, and when that doesn't work, you take more away from them. Although, I have no idea what that might be at this point." He just smiled, like he had a list of things he could do. "Oh, I need to hear this. What is it you have planned for them?"

"Your mom is going to help me with it, but I think we'll be able to rid the world of them once and for all." Danburn asked again. "We're going to strip them of their dragons."

"You can do that?" Hanson glanced at the Board members, who were nodding their heads and smiling. "I wasn't aware of this. How does that work?"

"I wasn't either, my lord." Shadberry, he thought his name was, flushed brightly. "Had it not been pointed out to us by Lord McClain's mate, we might not have ever known about it. She is most informed about things. We thought perhaps when this is finished we'd ask her to come help us with other matters. We've given her our copies of other dragon books, and she is reading them now."

Danburn laughed. It was funny to him that a human had been the one that told them how to deal with dragons. As they sat there, explaining things to him, he thought of something else. The books that he had, all of them, could be just as useful if someone knew what was in them. He mentioned that to Shadberry.

"Oh yes, that would be a wonderful idea. She has also expressed a desire to put them in the computer, to make sure that they're safe." He thought that was a splendid idea too. "She is brilliant, my lord. And very good at interpreting the rules for everyone to understand."

"I'm sure that she is." A thought occurred to him. "She can read them? The books I have here are in English, but yours…they're all in Latin, aren't they? And a few of them were written in dragon speak."

"She can read them all, but it wasn't until I pointed it out to her that she realized they weren't in English. I think, and I hope I'm right, that this is part of the magic she got from me as my mate." He looked at Hanson when he spoke. "I'm not sure how that happened, but I haven't had time to figure it out yet. That is just one theory that I'm working on. It's in the works. Right now, I'm dealing with my parents."

"Then we'll need to talk to her, and Carmine." Shadberry asked who that was. "Her sister, the Lady Quinn's baby sister that has been orphaned recently. She's come in contact with the McClains, and we need to keep her safe."

"Oh yes. Human children would never stand a chance against them. They'd gobble her up without any trouble." Danburn thought that was about right, but thought they could have worded it better. "When Lord Hanson goes to speak to them, you and your mother will be with him? It should be quite a thing, with them."

"We'll be there. You can count on it." Hanson hadn't told them the whole truth about Carmine, and Danburn decided that he was all right with that. The fewer people who knew about her, the safer she'd be. Not to mention, they didn't really know much right now, and that was another reason to keep it from them. He and Hanson set up a time after Shadberry and his aide left. It was about time someone dealt with these people.

Chapter 6

Edwin looked around the area and was quite pleased with himself. In a fit of rage he'd gone on a rampage, and had killed whatever got in his way. Well, he had gone looking for most of the things, so mostly it was animals that were there just minding their own business. But he'd killed without thought as to what the death of so many would mean to the area. One of the too numerous rules that had been laid out for their kind. This one dealt with the circle of life and how it needed to be balanced, and he'd taken it all out of kilter. A thing that every dragon had to be aware of when they fed was to kill only what they needed. Today was just killing because he could. When Geraldine returned from the lake, he asked her if she'd had fun.

"Yes. The water will never be the same after I had my bit of fun. To think that all this time we've been laying on that asshole's land and didn't even know it. Think of the damage we could have done had we more notice. Boiled fish smells terrible too, just in case you didn't know." She sat down and picked up the deer meat he'd put on the spit earlier. "I'm so glad that you had this idea, Edwin. It's very refreshing to have some fun at someone else's expense. Do you suppose that he'll figure out it was us?"

"I don't care." He didn't, either. It was a terrible thing, yes, but he'd been angry and had done it without thinking when he'd been upset. Besides, what were they going to do about it? Nothing. They'd messed up, and he'd say he was sorry and that would be the end of it. Danburn English could go straight to the Board for all he cared, but since there was nothing else they could take from them, he didn't care one whit.

"How's your arm?" It was still paining him, but with the fun he'd had, he'd forgotten about it for a time. He told her that it was healing, but too slowly for his tastes. "Did you know that Hanson could do that? I certainly didn't. I wonder where he got that little bit of magic? It would be useful on a great many things if he'd share it with us."

"You don't think he will any more than I do. Besides, I've been thinking on that. I don't think it was him anyway. I think it was that woman or her kid." Geraldine asked him which woman. "His supposed mate. The human female. And if he thinks for one moment that we didn't notice that, he's going to be in for a rude awakening."

"Focus, Edwin. Why do you think it was the human? I mean, they're human, yes? And for the most part, useless and without powers." He wanted to smack her for using that tone with him, but he only sat there until she either apologized to him or she hurt him. He was afraid it was going to be the latter of the two when she spoke again. "Tell me, or I shall enter your head with a rock and find it for myself."

She would too. Geraldine was violent when she was angry. Most of the time it wasn't aimed at him, but of late—

and he was sure it was because they only had each other as company — she'd been snapping and biting at him. And it was painful. Plus, it took so long to heal.

"When I pointed out to him that he was hurting me, he didn't even come to my aid. But he did kneel to the child. And yes, she is human, but there was something about her that made me think that she could do this thing anyway. Like the way she was staring at me from behind our son." She said she'd not noticed. "Yes, well, I've been much more observant than you have ever been, Geraldine, and you know it. But there is something there. Something that we should take care to find out about."

"We should take her." He'd been thinking the same thing. And if she wasn't the one that hurt him, then they'd use her to get what they wanted. They weren't above kidnapping to get their magic back. "How easy do you think it'll be to do that? I mean, they are pretty good at keeping her around people and such. And that pack, they're forever roaming the lands. Stinky wolves that do nothing more than fuck and eat. I swear to you, Edwin, our son is hanging around losers. And it's beginning to tick me off."

"Yes, but we have an added advance. We're her grandparents, correct?" She frowned at him and asked him how that was. "She's related to that female of his. The mate. So that makes us her — what does it matter how it works? It just does, darn it. Why do you have to make things so complicated all the time? I don't even know if I want to tell you my plan or not now, you've upset me so much."

"Tell me. I'm sorry. But you are rattling around a great deal without saying anything." He was, he supposed, but he was pulling out the suspense, something that she wouldn't get anyway. "Tell me, what is it you're thinking?"

"We introduce ourselves to her and have her come and visit us. We don't have anywhere to go, I know, but she won't know that, now will she? Anyway, after we get her in our hands, we'll call up Hanson and tell him what we want. He'll do it for the kid, and we'll get what we want too. Brilliant, don't you think?" She was shaking her head. "What is it now?"

"If, as you said, it was her that hurt you, I'm pretty sure that she'll know that we're not people to trust. And if that is so, then she's certainly not going to go anywhere with us. And not to mention, she's going to have heard that we don't have—"

"Do you have a better idea? If so, then I'd like to hear it." She said that she didn't, but was pointing out the mistakes that he'd made. "It was a work in progress, Geraldine, not a solid plan. I swear, you get meaner every day."

"Hello Father, Mother." They both stood up, and Edwin was ready to shift when he felt something curl around his dragon. He wasn't sure what was going on, but he couldn't call him forth. Their son had done this, he knew it. Or that English woman had. "I'd like to introduce you to my good friend, Danburn English, and his mother. I know that you've heard me talk about Danburn a great deal, but I don't remember if you've actually been—"

"We have met them. All of them. What is the meaning of this?" He wanted to ask Geraldine if she could call her dragon, but she was too busy yelling at Hanson. Edwin thought that might be a mistake right now. "We're not bothering anyone. Go away, unless you've come here to help us. We are your parents, you know."

"I'm well aware of what you are to me. And frankly, I couldn't care less, but as I was saying, you've never met

Danburn in his current title. He's Duke of Winchester, and King of the Dragons." Edwin wanted to deny the last thing he'd been called, but felt the truth of it all the way to his cock and balls. Which were, at this moment, curled up so tight he could feel them with his butthole. "And his lovely wife is the queen, Lady Kendrick. Would you like to know my title?"

"No, we would not." He nodded when his wife spoke, but she went on as if she was there to have them killed. "What I want to know is what you're planning on doing with this Board issue we have."

"You no longer have an issue with the Board." Edwin was so relieved that he had to have a seat. "You have a problem with me and the king."

"What sort of problem? You have nothing to say to us." He tried to get Geraldine to shut up, or at the very least leave him out of this. "You're our son, and there isn't any way you can do any more to us than the Board has already. Go away if you're not going to help us. But if you do, then you're nothing to us. Not that you have been anyway, but we'd disown you."

"You've destroyed animals here on my land. You've taken away the fish that feed the others here, myself and my family included. You've soiled the land with death, and the blood of creatures that you have not eaten. That alone has you in trouble with me." Danburn stared at them both until Edwin wanted to crawl away with his tail, quite literally, between his legs. "I will sentence you first."

"No you won't." Edwin looked at his mate and wondered who had taken control of her mouth and body. She was going to get them both killed, and he wasn't sure that wasn't her plan. He tried to pull her back. "Edwin, leave me be. I've got this. This is nothing more than a misunderstanding on their part. We were angered, as you said, and took it out on the area. I'm sorry. There, now what can you do to us? Nothing, that's what. So long as we tell the injured party that we've made a mistake and are sorry for it, it's done. I do know that."

"You are hereby ordered to replace every blade of grass that you ruined. Return the waterways to their original state. You will replenish the seed that has been killed in the animals and families that have been harmed. You will do this, or I shall take the highest form of repayment from you." Geraldine looked at Edwin, then back at Danburn before laughing. It was loud and manic, like she didn't believe this man. "You will do this?"

"No. I don't even know how you'd think we could, much less think we would do it. We're royalty, not slaves to you. We don't have to do anything, I don't care who you say you are." Danburn said something like "So be it," but he wasn't sure that was right. It sounded like he was just going to let it go. He should have known better.

He felt it, the pain that was just a little more painful than the one at his wrist. Then as his nose started to bleed, he looked at Geraldine when she screamed. Something was happening. The pain was too much, but not enough to knock him out. But the longer he sat there, his body no longer able to support himself, the more he thought they should have run when they could. They were in trouble here, more so than he thought that the Board would have done. And their son was letting it happen to them.

"What is this?" He wanted to know too, but was in no position to ask as Geraldine had. As the pain became more unbearable, he felt the blood rushing over his face, so much so that he was blinded by it. And when he was flat upon the ground, all he could do was look at the man who was indeed their king.

"Now, it's my turn." Hanson only lifted his hands and said something in their old language. It had been so very long since he'd spoken it that it took him several seconds to realize what he was saying. He was taking their dragons?

"You will forever walk the earth as humans. You will both feel all of the pain of a mortal when you are harmed. You will die when your time comes, and nothing will save you. The dragons that you abused have been given to others, their lives now in the bodies of people much more deserving. People that will care for the dragons' needs before their own. Edwin and Geraldine McClain, you will no longer have the magic that you once abused. Now and forever, you will be nothing to any of us."

Edwin knew the moment when he no longer had a beast to call upon. He was weak with the loss of him. And when he searched for him, calling for him to come back to his body, there was nothing there. It was as if he'd never had him, never called upon him to be there for him. As he lay there, his body burning with pain and a desire to die now, he looked up at the child he'd seen earlier.

He had no idea why she frightened him so much. She was a little thing, no bigger than his nails when he was a dragon, but terrified of her he was. So much so that he curled from her, backing away even though the pain was more than he'd ever felt.

"You're a bad man." He couldn't even disagree with her. "I'm sending you away. Don't come back here."

When he opened his eyes, without even realizing that he'd closed them, he was in a cell, like a dungeon under the ground where he'd put so many people before. Sitting up slowly, his body riddled with newfound pain, he couldn't find his mate. He was alone.

"Geraldine? My love, where are you?" Nothing. Not even a little sliver of knowledge that she was nearby. Calling to her again and again, he knew that she was dead. The loss of connection with her was so profound, that could be the only reason for it. Edwin wanted to die…without her there beside him, he had no will to go on.

There was no link to her. He could see her face in his mind and knew it as well as his own, but he could no longer reach out to her. Like his dragon, it was as if she had never been a part of him. Not loved him, nor bore any children for them. As he leaned against the wall of his cell, he sobbed.

"Geraldine, where are you?" His voice sounded so hollow. Pain now centered around his heart. He was alone. More alone than he'd ever been in his entire life. And because of his son. "Hanson, if you can hear me, I'm so sorry. About everything." Nothing. He tried again. "I'll make it up to you, if you'd allow it. I'd like to start new. And I won't even beg you for my dragon back yet. Please, come and get me out of here." He sat there for hours calling for anyone that would come to his aid, but nothing nor anyone did. "Hanson?"

As the sun bled out of the room and the darkness took its place, he never heard from anyone. Food appeared before him but he didn't touch it. And when it disappeared, he didn't even bother putting up a fuss. Edwin wondered when this would all end, and closed his eyes when the light once again began to fill the dark spaces.

~~~

"Carmine, how are you able to do that?" She didn't answer her sister, just ate her dinner without looking up. "Carmine, no one is going to be upset with you."

"Yes, you will. You'll say that because you want me to tell you, but you don't really want me to because I make you nervous." She knew that to be true, just like she knew that they were dragons. No one had told her, but she knew. "That man wasn't nice, and I was afraid he was going to hurt you guys. Isn't that enough for you?"

"Where are they?" Carmine looked at Hanson and he asked her again. "You sent them away. While I have no idea how you did that, I know that you did it to protect us. Where are they now?"

"A dungeon, like they put your sister in when they thought she was being bad, but not really. They're in a cell together, but they don't know it. They can't hear or feel each other." He nodded but didn't say anything. Putting down her fork, she used her powers to lift the roast that was on the platter in the center of the table. "I can do all kinds of things with my brain. Mom knew some of it, but not all. She tried to protect me too. No one is going to be able to take this from me, not like you did the dragons, but I have it all the same. I'm sorry."

"Don't be sorry, love. I'm not the least bit upset that you did this or about what you can do. But this dungeon that they're in, where is it? My house?" She told him it wasn't real either. "I don't understand."

"They're in a place that I made up. There is a cell, but it's in a building that no one goes to and has been empty and forgotten for a long time. Their heads think that they're apart and they can't hear each other, but as I said, they are only a few feet apart. I won't let them starve or anything, but they can't get out, ever." He nodded, and she wondered if he was okay with that. "You can't make me let them out. They'll come back."

"Yes, they would, and you can leave them wherever they are. I don't want them to harm anyone." She put the roast down and he looked at it. "You're very strong, aren't you?"

"Yes. I can do a lot of things. The hospital, they said that it was because I have a big brain." He nodded and smiled at her. "Are you going to sell me off?"

"Sell you off? No. Why would you even...? Who tried to sell you off, Carmine? Your mom? Someone else?" She nodded at him and waited. He was much smarter than she'd thought he was. "Who was it?"

"The teachers at the school where I was at." He asked her what she'd done to them. "Nothing. I tried to make them forget, but I didn't know how then. I do now, but it's too late. There are a lot of people who know."

"Are they coming after you?" She nodded and played with her food as Quinn continued. "And these people, they're going to try and take you with them to have you do things for them. You know this?"

"Yes. They think I can control guns and satellite dishes." Quinn asked her if she could. "Yes. It's easy. Especially since I've come here with you."

"The magic of the land." Carmine wanted them to stop asking questions, but she had known this was coming. She'd also been told to answer their questions truthfully so that they'd not be afraid of her. "Danburn said that the land here is magical and that it feeds every living creature here. Including their magic."

"I won't hurt any of you guys. Not ever. You know that, don't you?" They both said that they did. She believed them. "And Danburn and his family...I won't hurt them either. They're good people."

"Yes, they are. All of them are." She knew that too. "Do you know what we are, Carmine? I mean, any of us?"

"Yes. I know what creatures are as soon as I see them. I

88

used to have to touch them, but that's not necessary anymore. I just see it. Like the guy that was here today, Shadberry. He's not a dragon, but he rules them. He's a good man too." Hanson said that was right. "And there is a vampire too; she's nearby, but not here. There is something holding her back from making you guys know her."

"A vampire? Here?" Carmine told him that she was hiding from her maker, but would soon come to them for help. "And should we help her?"

"Yes. She is going to be very helpful when the men come here for me." Quinn took her hand in hers; it was warm and comforting. "I won't let them hurt you, Sissy. I promise you that I'll make sure you are safe."

"I want you to know that I'll do the same for you." She looked at Hanson, and he looked so serious she believed him. "I wanted to talk to you about what it is you can do. I know that you can control things with your mind, but I think that there is more, isn't there?"

"Yes." She waited, not to put him off, but because she wasn't sure how to tell him. Instead, she decided to show them both. With just a thought, she moved the three of them to the living room. Hot tea and scones were there in front of them, and a fire in the fireplace. "There is more. Can I show you?"

"Yes, always." She nodded, not showing off, but afraid that they'd be scared of her. Her mom had been, she knew that. "What are you thinking about, honey?"

"That you'll hate me. That you won't want me here." He said that he'd never do that. And Quinn said that she loved her and could never hate her. "Okay, but you have to go to the window."

They both went to the window and she let her mind work.

89

In moments she knew what they were seeing, and could feel their awe as well as their confusion. The pool just beyond them started to fill, the water as clear as the sky above and warm enough for them to enjoy even though it was only in the thirties outside.

"That's wonderful." She got up and went to the window with them. She was sure that they weren't seeing what she had meant for them to. "The pool will be ready for us in the spring. Can we use it now too?"

"Yes. It'll adjust the temperature to suit you." She looked up at them both. "You know what I'm doing? That I've filled the pool with the water from the earth and warmed it? I did that."

"I can see that. It's wonderful." Hanson knelt down to her level, much like he'd done when his parents had shown up. "We don't discourage magic or whatever it is that you can do around here, love. But we want you to be careful who you show it to. All right?"

She nodded and looked at her sister when she came to her level too. "You're my baby sister, and will forever be that. You have a talent that we're all learning about, so we want you to be careful, like Hanson said. Practice here as much as you want, so long as you don't hurt yourself or others. But in the public eye, be very careful. All right?"

She said that she would and sat back down. Carmine hadn't ever thought that they'd be this accepting of what she'd done. Her mom hadn't been, and it had hurt her. But she knew that Quinn and Hanson weren't afraid of her, and that made her smile.

Going up to bed later that night, she wasn't surprised to find someone in her room. Danielle was there, and she looked afraid. Sitting on the bed, she waited for her to come out of the shadows, and when she sat down on the chair, she asked her if she was all right.

"I am. Are you well?" She told her what she'd done for her sister and her mate. "They took it well then? They are not upset with you?"

"No. They said that I had to be careful not to show too many people. They're worried about those men." Danielle said she was as well. "I told you, they don't know about you. But they are coming for me."

"I shall be here if you should need me." Carmine nodded. She knew that they all would be. "You told them of me? They know that I am around?"

"Yes. They're very nice people. I don't think that anyone would harm you. When are you coming to see them?"

As Danielle always did, she ignored the question with one of her own. "The dragons that were here, you've taken care of them?" She told her what Danburn and the others had done. Then she explained to her what she'd done. "Danburn is the dragon king. His mate carries a child that will rule someday as well. She is but a girl child, but will rule."

"I don't think they care what your gender is like vampires do." She nodded. Carmine knew her story, that her family thought her unworthy. "They don't know that you're here, Danielle. I promise you that they don't."

"I know you say that, but they can find me. Or order me home." They couldn't, and she told her that again. "You can say that, but I find it hard to believe a child. I am sorry, but to me you are but a babe. I am hundreds of years old."

"I know, but you have to believe me, and in them." Danielle told her to rest now. She was there to watch over her. "Please, go and talk to Danburn. Or my sister. She'll know what to do about them."

"I will think on it. You rest. You have much to do tomorrow." She was going to school for the first time since moving here. "I have checked over the school where you will be going. You know that he is the first wolf? The one that all shifter wolves are made from? He is a good man, one that you can trust. And his pack, they're not like others...they are there for each other and are very good men and women. If you are in trouble there, you go to them and listen. They will keep you safe when I cannot. As I told you, little one, I cannot go into the hottest part of the day, it will kill me."

She hadn't known about Shawn, but she did like the man. He was a handsome wolf, and his pack was huge. Carmine also knew that she'd be safe there, as safe as she was here. After laying down, she heard Danielle humming.

"What is that? The song?" She told her that her mother had sang it to her brother. "But not to you? That's so sad. I think it's beautiful."

"Go to sleep, young miss." Laughing, she rolled to her side. Closing her eyes, she heard Danielle once again humming and fell asleep to the music. She did have things going on tomorrow, and needed the rest.

Chapter 7

Ramon Packer looked over the map and tried to pinpoint the last known whereabouts of the kid. It didn't matter if he lived in the same town for years, he couldn't find his way without landmarks guiding him. Or a map. Having access to things like records and shit like that for his job helped him a great deal. Who would have ever thought that being a paranormal investigator would be so helpful or financially rewarding?

He knew she was around…her mom had died around here someplace, the obit in the paper had said. But it had been a real bitch trying to find out where the hell the little girl was. And having like ten thousand kids in town shopping for school shit was making it even harder.

"Did you know that there are four local schools around here? And that all of them have open registration?" He asked him why he'd care. "Because even if you found out what district the kid is living in, she could be going to any one of them. They don't care here where you live so long as they have the classroom size for you."

"And again, why do I care? We're looking for a new kid that goes here with the last name of Langley. Should narrow it down a good bit, don't you think?" His son, Ramon Junior, going by Ramie, shook his head. "What the fuck are you trying so very hard to annoy me with?"

"Here you go. I picked this up at the local schoolboard meeting. It's the names of all the kids that are going to start this week after the break, and what classrooms still need teacher helpers." He looked it over, and was shocked by the number of names on the list. "There are currently twenty-six girls with the first name of Carmine, and twelve kids with the last name of Langley. I counted both in the event that they changed their last name for some reason, and then I counted Langleys in case they didn't. That is a shitload of kids to find. And guess what? Not any of them are Carmine Langley."

"This is just a little bump in the road for us. We'll get to the schools and find her during one of those breaks. Or, we might just have to set a few fires to have all the brats coming out of the classroom at once, and snatch us up a few just to make sure we get the right one." He handed him a photo of the girl. "I got this from her momma when she was worried about her. I never dreamed when she called me up for a little sit down that she had the real deal with her daughter. It's a real shame that she didn't want to play ball with us and sell her. But we'll get it taken care of."

He hoped so. Ramon had two people that he wanted to take the kid to see. Both of them military, and both very wealthy. They were going to make him a very rich man. Ramie asked if he had called back his employer.

"You might need something to fall back on should this fall through. I'm not saying it will, Dad, but the money will come in handy when Margie has the baby." He nodded, not caring a fig about his son's girlfriend or the baby that she was going to squirt out. Ramon had a feeling that it wasn't his son's anyway, and wasn't going to help them out by paying for shit the kid would ruin the first time it put them on. If there even was a kid at all, which he wholly believed that there wasn't. "Margie said she's picked out a nice bed and dresser for him. I need some money to put it in layaway."

"Do I have *bank* written on my forehead? Do you see a slot where a credit card will fit in my wallet? You know why you don't see it? Because there ain't no fucking slot or bank on my head. Why the hell doesn't she get herself a job and pay for that shit on her own? For that matter, why don't you have a job? You could be paying for that kid all on your own if you did." Ramie pouted. He was a grown fucking man at twenty-six, and he acted most of the time like he was ten and needed a time out. "You want my help? Then you help yourself. I'm not taking you in to raise again, Ramie. Nor that kid of yours. Is it even yours?"

"She said it was." That made him want to smack his son hard enough up the side of his head to knock some sense into him. But Ramon didn't think it would work. He was just too dumb. "You don't want a grandchild, Dad?"

"If it's yours, yes. But you don't sound so sure if it is or not." He told him again that she said it was his. "Yeah? Well, does she lead you around by your pecker or your nose, Ramie? Either way, you gotta start thinking like a man, not some kid that had his dick watered and now doesn't have brain cell one."

"Dad, you gonna talk like that around the baby?" He told him he'd talk any way he wanted. "Yeah, well, maybe we won't let you babysit it. How about that?"

"Suits me just fucking fine and dandy. I don't want to

95

babysit no snot nosed little fucker anyway." His son shook his head and walked away. "If that's all it takes, then fuck fuckity fuck."

When his son was gone again, he pulled out the list. If someone would have bothered to ask him, he'd have thought that this place wasn't big enough to handle so many schools. And then to hand out a list of kids like it was a Christmas list was something that he'd think was wrong too. But then again, he'd not been asked about it. Going through the lists, he noticed a school name that had nothing listed.

Looking on his computer, the Luna Private School was just that, private. There wasn't an address for the place, or phone numbers that he could find. There wasn't even a website listed for the place. Just the name and the fact that it was private.

"How the hell do they do that? I mean seriously, how does Mom call in for little Jack when he's sick?" He tried to call one of the other schools on the list and was told that they'd be open on Monday. "But I just want to find out a number for the Luna School."

"I'm sorry, sir, but there isn't a number that I can give you." He asked her if she wouldn't or couldn't. "I don't have one. They're a private school funded by their own money. They've been known to have good school activities and such, but they are very private."

After she hung up on him when he'd asked her several times for a number, he sat in his chair and stared at the computer. He had no idea why, but he thought that was where he was going to find the kid. Private or not, he was going to find out the information that he needed and go in there and get her. And when he did, he'd have enough money to make his own little private place.

Ramon looked at the picture again. She was a good looking kid. Blonde hair and dark eyes. He'd never been sure if they were blue or black when he'd had the one occasion to see her face to face, but he was sure they were dark because they were from the depths of hell. The one time he'd seen her was what convinced him that she was going to do all right for him.

He'd been watching for her walking home from school. It had taken him the better part of two weeks to get the mother to tell him where she'd gone. When she'd called to ask questions of his firm about what would happen to her little girl if anyone found out that she could lift things with just her mind, he'd been the one to catch the call. Lucky for him. Not so much for Momma and her kid, he thought.

"What do you mean, she can lift things? You mean, she's strong?" She'd told him that she wasn't, but that she would lift things from across the room to her without touching them. "Little things, or bigger? Like a book or something bigger?"

"Much bigger if she's a mind to. Like the other day, she lifted up the couch when I was sweeping. I needed to get under it, and she helped me out. What would happen to her should someone find out? Would they take her from me?" He told her that he wouldn't think so, and turned off the recording device on his phone. "She's my little girl, and I don't want anything to happen to her."

"Of course you don't. And I don't either." He asked her where she went to school. "I should have extra people put there to keep her safe."

She never told him then, or later that night when he called her back. So, over the next several days, he'd called her back several times a day, every day, to get any information he could.

That day, he'd been hanging out at the school just waiting for her to do something. Float a bus or something, just so he could see what she was made of. Carmine had stared at him when she came out of the school...just stared at him like she knew what he was doing there and what he was thinking. When Ramon waved at her through the front of his car, she waved back and he could feel the car shake...like she had put her hand over his car and shaken him like one of those glass balls with snow in it.

Then alarms went off around him. Cars were shaking, the light above his head began to spark. About the time he started to get out of his car in case the light fell, his car started to squeeze together.

His doors smashed against him on both sides. The front glass, near where she was standing, blew out so that he could see her clearly. Then the tires blew out, all four of them. The spare under the mat in the back blew up; junk that was back there hit him in the head and flew out the missing window. Then she turned her back on him and everything stopped.

Ramon sat there for several minutes. Not that he could have gotten out of the car, but he did want to think. If she had done that to his car without so much as touching him, he wondered what she could do if she was really upset. Or being paid.

Then a couple of days later he'd been by the house again, and there wasn't anyone there. It was about then that he'd read about a Langley being shot to hell at the county offices, and he had to do some research on it but found out that it was the same family. Now he was looking for them again.

"Where are you? You hiding from me?" He smiled as he continued talking to himself. "You just think all you want that you have it all figured out. But I'm a man and you ain't nothing but a kid, and I'm a lot smarter."

As he started to put his things away, the files and the pictures that he'd been able to take of the kid before she took off, he heard his son in the other room with the girlfriend. They were bickering again. He'd thought it was fighting, but he'd been assured that they'd been bickering. Whatever the hell the difference was, they were doing it again.

Margie Shaw was older than his son…he thought by fifteen years or more. But when he'd done a little research on her, he'd found out that she was nearly his age. More than twenty-five years older than him. And it put him to wondering if there even was a kid. She was a might long in the tooth, he thought, for that.

When his door burst open and the old broad was standing there, he looked at his son, standing just behind her. He had a feeling that she was going to say something dumb right now, and he turned his back on her. She didn't have shit to say to him.

"You gonna help us out with this kid?" He didn't bother answering her. "There are sales going on right now, and I need some money to get them. Unless you want to pay full price for them. Is that it, you too proud to buy on sale? What an idiot you are. How about you give me the full price for them, I'll get the ones on sale, and put the rest of the money to good use? For your grandchild. I need that money."

"Get you a job then." He wasn't sure what she'd hit him with, but his head exploded in pain. "What the fuck is wrong with you? Get the fuck out of here."

Ramie was dragging her back when Ramon sat down on his chair. His hand came away covered in blood, and he stared at it while she screamed at him to give her some money. That woman was nuts, he thought, and when his son figured that out, he'd be better off.

When the door shut to the front of the house, Ramie came back to his office, telling him he was sorry. Showing him the blood on his hand, Ramon snorted when Ramie again said he was sorry. Ramon didn't want sorry, he wanted her out of his life.

"She's old, did you know that? I mean, she could be my sister, she's that old." Ramie said she was only four years older than him. Ramon pulled the birth certificate out and handed it to him. "This ain't her, Dad. This is her mom. It's gotta be. Margie, she's not that old."

"No, son, it's her. She shaved a few years off her year of birth, but that's her. And if she's gonna lie about her age, then I'm betting she's lying about a lot of shit." He asked if he meant the baby. "Yes. You trust me, go to the next appointment with her and find out. You find out the truth and come back here and tell me. But I'm betting that it's all a lie."

"All right, Dad. But if I do and find out that she's not lying, then you have to be nicer to her." He pointed out that she'd hit him in the head. "Yeah, but it's hormones, she told me. She's under a lot of stress. You know how that is."

He didn't, but he wasn't going to get into a big debate with his moron son. The kid needed to have his own head checked out. If he thought he was ever going to be nice to this woman, then all hell was going to break lose.

~~~

Hanson walked along the path that looked as if it had been there for more years than he'd been coming around to see Danburn. When he was deep in the woods, he let his dragon take him. He needed some time as his beast so that he could fly the skies and forget life for a while. As soon as he felt the first rain drops touch him, he took to the clouds.

You care if I join you? He told Cassie to come along. *Thank you. I wasn't sure that anyone would be out here. I wanted to blow some human off me.*

I know that feeling. They flew the skies for a little over an hour, then he spoke to her again. *I'm thinking of my sister today. It would have been her birthday.*

And yours too, I guess. He said that his was tomorrow. *Ah. Well, happy birthday tomorrow. Why are you thinking of your sister now? I mean, something happen?*

My parents are gone. They both died yesterday afternoon. No one did it, they just succumbed to their age. Carmine had told him right after they died, within minutes of each other. *She brought their bodies here, and I'm going to bury them on the back of the property.*

I'm sorry for your loss. He thanked her. *But they were never very nice to you, were they? I don't mean to belittle your pain, but I'd think you'd think it was a good thing.*

It is, in a way, a relief to have them gone. I don't have to worry about them coming around and hurting the family. But they were my parents. I'm sorry, I'm not explaining this very well. She said that he was doing fine. *They were horrible people. They murdered my sister, and a great many other people too. And would have any of us had they been able to get close enough.*

So, it's a good thing. He supposed it was. *You're thinking of this all wrong. Don't think of them as dead, but away from you forever. The same thing, but not quite so final.*

They didn't speak about his parents for the rest of their time in the sky, but they did talk about the coming holiday. The trees that were going to be put up, as well as shopping trips. When she left him a bit later, he landed in the same woods and saw Quinn there. She was sitting on a large boulder and waiting for him.

101

"You been here long?" Quinn told him that she'd been watching him. "I'm sorry. You should have told me and I would have come back."

"No, it's fine. And I enjoyed myself." He sat beside her. "You okay? When you said you were coming out here, I had a feeling that you needed to get away from us. I told you that it was too much to have me and a little girl in your house."

"No, it wasn't that at all. I just needed to think about my parents and their deaths." Quinn nodded. "I love you. I need you to know that more than anything. And it's never too much to have you both there. I'm loving having my two favorite women in the house."

"She was telling me about her new school today. I guess she had a good class day, and she also said that she is supposed to be tested next week for upper classes she can take." He told her that was wonderful. "They're a very progressive school setting, aren't they?"

"Yes. Instead of teaching one grade, they have different rooms for the kids to learn in. Some of them are upperclassmen, and there are even classes that they can teach too. It's a very hands on sort of environment." He pulled her to his lap and held her. "However, I love this class that you and I have right now. Where I can have some hands on with you."

She turned on his lap so that she was facing him. It was nice, having her there, and he started to unbutton her blouse while she spoke. He wasn't sure what she was talking about, he wasn't really paying attention, but when he lifted his head up so that he was looking at her, she smiled.

"You didn't hear a word I just said to you, did you?" He said that he'd been distracted. "Yes, I've noticed that about you. You get that way very easily."

"Only when you're around, I do." He pulled her closer

to him and suckled at her breast before speaking again. "Of course, I could distract you too if you want. It'll be a nice thing to be distracted together, don't you think?"

When she was naked, he stood up and told her to lean against the tree. He was going to take her there, but first he wanted to drink from her. And when he got down on his knees in front of her, he could smell her need, see it as her juices ran down her legs.

"You're beautiful when you're like this. Spread out for me like a feast. Your body so warm and ready for mine." He slid his fingers up her leg and gathered her cream before taking his fingers to his mouth. "Just as delicious as I thought it would be. And all mine."

He ate her for as long as she let him. Her screams were like music to his ears every time she came. And when she begged him to let her rest, he laid her out on the ground and continued what he'd been doing, enjoying her as much as he could.

"Please, Hanson, take me, please?" He moved up her body, nipping and licking her everyplace that he could. When he got to her mouth, he kissed her hungrily as he slid home. Her body was tight, her cream making him slide into her deeply. "You fill me. Not just with your body, but with everything you are. And I love you so very much."

He took her then, not hard but gently, making love to her until they were both sated, their bodies fulfilled. As he lay there with his arm around her, he felt the earth move under his fingers, and then something filled his palm. Pulling whatever it was from the earth, he heard the voice.

You are a good man, Hanson McClain. And a better dragon. He thanked the earth and told her that he was humbled that she'd speak to him. When he looked at Quinn, he knew that

103

she could hear her as well. *I have a gift for you both. Something that I have made myself for a couple such as you.*

"Thank you, my lady, but you don't need to give us anything. We're just happy that you allow us to use what you offer us." She told him it was her pleasure. "Thank you again."

He opened his palm and saw something shiny as he began to pull the dirt free of it. He had a feeling that he knew what it was going to be, and wasn't surprised to find a ring. What did startle him was how beautiful it was, and that it had a ruby that was as dark as the blood in his veins.

You will wear it, my lady? It has special powers to keep you safe. There is a smaller one for your sister to use. The ground moved again, and there on the top of it lay a bracelet of the same hue and stone. *She will need it in the coming months.*

Hanson slipped the ring on Quinn's finger, and smiled when it fit her like it had been made for her, and he supposed in a way that it had been. And when she sat up, he helped her find her clothing so they could head back to the house. But the earth stopped him once more.

The dragons, my lord, do you know where they have gone? He told her that Danburn had said they went to someone more deserving. *Yes, I believe that they have. Good luck, my lord. I do hope Ladies Quinn and Kendrick enjoy them.*

He was nearly to the house when what she had said occurred to him. Hanson stopped walking and looked at Quinn. The earth had asked him where the dragons had gone because she knew already, and wondered if he did. When Quinn turned back and asked him what was wrong, he could only smile. She had the dragon. He didn't know why he knew that, but he was sure that was what the lady of the earth had meant.

104

Instead of asking Quinn about it, he reached for Danburn. Telling him what was just told to him, he felt his laughter before he spoke again.

Yes, she is one. I didn't give it to her, but gave the dragons to the earth so that they could use the magic from them. Danburn laughed harder. *Kendrick is now, as we speak, using hers to walk around the yard. It is the most comical thing I've ever seen. But I'll not tell her that. She isn't going to be happy with me if she finds out.*

He told Quinn that she was a dragon now. And when she shook her head at him, he told her to think of one, look deep inside of herself and find her. When she closed her eyes and then opened them quickly, he knew that she'd seen her. And when she asked how she became her, he told her. In seconds, Quinn was walking around the yard as a large ruby red dragon.

I want to soar with you. He asked her if she was ready for that. *Yes, I'm so ready for this. I want to fly with you.*

She soared upward and then landed gently. Over and over again she took off for the highest cloud, only to return a few minutes later. He asked her what she was doing, and she said she was getting used to her. Then she asked him to come with her. He wondered how well Kendrick was doing when they made their way to Danburn's castle.

She wasn't as far along as Quinn was. She could fly, but her landing was nearly a disaster every time she came down. He laughed once, and that was all it took for her to turn on him with her flames roaring at him. Hanson thought it was the funniest thing he'd ever seen, having a little bitty flame racing toward him, only to peter out before it touched him. Of course, that pissed her off more.

It wasn't until they were all human again, wearing their clothing just as he and Danburn did when they shifted, that he noticed Kendrick's ring. Her dragon was the same color as her ring, just as Quinn's was. The lady earth had been planning this for some time, he thought.

Chapter 8

He'd found her. Ramon danced around the little office he'd been in for five minutes before he sat down. Christ, it had taken the better part of a week to find the kid, and now he had her. Ramon was going to go then and find the brat when his son came in and sat down across from him. He asked him what was going on. He just knew he was going to fuck up his plans for his night. Ramie had that sullen childish look about him.

"I asked if I could go to the doctor with her, and she told me it was a girl thing. That I'd be bored and that I'd drive her crazy. I asked her, Dad, nicely too." He started to tell his son to grow some balls, but he continued before he could. "So I followed her. I borrowed a car and followed her to what I thought was a doctor's office. Do you know where she was? What she was doing? Huh, Dad? You know?"

"No, but I'm betting you're going to tell me." His son got up and started pacing. And bawling. It was worse than having a little kid around when he got like this. Acting like he was a baby when he was a grown assed man. "Ramie, just fucking tell me."

"She was gambling, betting the money that I gave her for the doctor's appointment today on slots." Ramon didn't say anything; he was wondering where his son had gotten money to give the bitch when he sat down again. "After I saw her go in there, I went to the doctor that she said she was going to. I had to find him, but when I saw the office building that she had me take her to the first time, it was all closed up. Like nothing had ever been there. So I made some calls to the places that she told me she had to go. You know, for blood work and stuff. You were right."

"I told you I was. And did you talk to her? Did you confront her?" He shook his head. "Then what the hell did you do that for if you wasn't going to talk to her about it? Damn it son, what am I going to do with you?"

"I killed her." Ramon didn't move. Didn't even let the breath out that had gotten stuck in his lungs. "She was coming out of the offices like she'd been there all along, and I shot her in the head. She's dead, Dad. I had to do it. She wasn't going to scam me and get away with it."

"Did anyone see you?" He said that he didn't think so. "You don't think so? That's the same as saying that someone did see you. Where is the body right now?"

"Right where she was coming out of the place. Her body fell back into the building, but I just left her there after I closed the door on her. I didn't touch her. I didn't even know the gun was in the car until I saw her. I was looking for something to write her a note, then I'd seen her when I found it." He asked him who the car had belonged to. "I don't know. I just borrowed it from the parking lot."

There could have been cameras there. The gun would have his prints on it. Also, and here was the biggy, anyone at all could have seen him coming or going. Or shooting the bitch. Christ, this had nightmare written all over it.

"Nobody saw me, Dad, I promise you. And I took the car back and wiped it down. There ain't no cameras there. Remember the store over on Hudson? You know the one. I used to work there. They ain't got no camera at all." That took care of some of it, but not all. "I even remembered to take the gun with me, and I put it in that wet concrete that they're pouring over at the new mall."

"You done this before, son?" He shook his head and said he watched television. "You do, do you? Well then, you know them people always get themselves caught, don't they? Otherwise they'd not be showing it on television. Christ oh mighty, Ramie, this is bad. Real bad. And if she was carrying your kid like she told you, then—"

"There ain't no baby. She told me that when I confronted her." Now he'd talked to her? This was as fucked up as it came. And he wasn't going down for anything that his son did. "I don't want to go to jail, Dad, but I think I did everything I could think to do so that I don't. But she lied to me."

"Yeah, women lie all the time. All the fucking time, and while that's as true as it comes, there ain't no law that's going to save your ass for killing her for it. Mother fuck." And here he'd been in a good mood because he'd found out where the kid was. "You have to turn yourself in."

"No, I don't want to do that. I don't want to go to jail. Think of something else. How about I go away and not come back?" Ramon thought of all the things that would do for him. No sharing of the money collected for the brat. No one breathing down his neck asking what he could do now for him. And certainly no moping around the fucking house saying how some woman lied to him. "I could just run off, and when nobody looks for me, then I can come back. That way, you and me, we can do this thing with the kid."

"Yeah, yeah, I think that might work. You can call me sometimes, you know, once a month or so, and I can tell you if anyone is looking for you. You know, I like that idea." He walked his son to his room. "Don't take a lot of stuff. Just enough to get you by for a month. You know, all your underwear and shirts. A few pair of jeans."

"I don't have any money." He did, but he wasn't sure that giving it to his son, a murderer, was such a good idea. "Just enough to get me away, Dad. I'll find me work and then I'll have my own."

"Okay." He gave him all the cash he had on him, just over five hundred dollars. "You find you work fast, that way you can come home when it's time. And then I won't have to be sending you money all the time. I'm sure that those shows you watch, it had that in them some place."

"Yeah, and burner phones. You should get one of those for us. Nobody can trace them, I guess." He was sure that that's what the police wanted you to think about them, but he only nodded. "I'm so sorry, Dad. You can't imagine what I was thinking when I saw what she'd done to me."

His son left an hour later. He'd even packed all the food that he could carry, as well as a credit card that Ramon had been holding onto for a while now that he'd taken from some kid at a store one day. After Ramon gave Ramie instructions, having him repeat them back several times, Ramie was gone. Ramon sat down on the couch and thought about what he'd just done.

"Good Christ, I just aided and abetted a criminal."

Laughing, he went to his kitchen again and started dinner. If his mom was here now, she'd have a fit on it. Then she'd make sure that Ramie had not just the food from the cabinet, but the freezer too.

Ramon went to bed just after midnight. He watched the news as well as the local shit, and heard not one word about the woman. Margie wasn't much liked, he knew that, but she was dead, and dead would draw anyone's attention, he figured.

Watching the morning news, he heard about a body being found in the lower north side, and that they were holding her name until they could find the next of kin. There wasn't any way to know if it was her or not, but he watched not just the morning news but had the radio and the scanner on too. He didn't hear anything until the noon news. By then, he was a wreck of nerves.

"The body of Margaret Shaw was discovered late yesterday afternoon. She'd been shot once in the head and left for dead." He was afraid that they were going to say that she was alive, but the newscaster, standing in front of an old abandoned building, said that she was deceased. "There are no suspects at this time, but the police are ruling this as a robbery gone wrong. A homicide."

By the time the six o'clock news came on, he was sick. He'd been watching every news program that came on the air for over twenty-four hours, and was so sick of hearing the weatherman talking about the cold and snow that he wanted to hunt him down and shoot him. Christ.

The eleven news had more information. Margie had been shot by an old lover, they thought. It wasn't the first time that there had been trouble from this woman. She'd been scamming men about her being with child for several years. The newscaster said they thought that things had finally caught up to her. Then they moved on to another story about

111

a kid who invented something to do with lost dogs.

Was that it? Did they not want to find the murderer because she'd been a terrible person? He had no idea, but when his phone rang a bit later, he screamed, it had startled him so much. When he heard Ramie on the line, he decided that he didn't need to know everything, not just yet, and told him that they were still looking for her murderer.

"You think they know it was me?" He told his son that he didn't know, only that the news said it was a former lover. "I think she had a lot of them, Dad. She seemed to know a lot of men."

"Yes, well, I told you she was bad news, didn't I? Right from the start, I told you that. And what if I had paid for all that shit she wanted? Huh? Where would I have been then?" He said he was sorry. "You'd best be hiding out and finding you a job. I got no money to be sending you any every time you get that dick of yours where it ain't supposed to be."

"I know. I'm so sorry, Dad." He told him to just stay away. "You find that girl yet? I think that will go a long way for me and you to get us some money, don't you think?"

"You let me worry about that girl. You just worry about keeping yourself from being arrested. There ain't enough money in the world for me to bail you out if you get your ass caught. You remember that." He said that he would. "Don't be calling here every day, Ramie. You do and they might know it. Just lay low and don't call me unless it's an emergency. All right?"

After hanging up, he laid in his bed. It was scary, thinking how stupid his son had been about this. And dumber still that Margie thought she could get away with it so many times. As he made notes on things he had to do tomorrow, he felt better.

He liked lists...it was following them that gave him

trouble. But he had to do this one, because if he got all messed up about things, then he'd be in prison. Or worse yet, he'd be dead for not delivering the kid.

The kid was going to give him fits, he had no doubt about that. He would have to get him something to drug her with to keep her quiet. And some kid food. He thought that she'd eat what his immature son ate, and that would narrow things down. The list of shit that he had to do was longer than his list to do on a regular day.

He felt like he'd done everything that he could. Going to the school tomorrow wasn't going to be easy. He figured that getting into a private place was going to need finesse. And Ramon had a great deal of that. He just hoped that the people running the place weren't some backwoods guitar playing fools that would just as soon shoot him as talk to him. Shaking his head, he turned out the light and went to sleep.

~~~

Shawn hated to ask her to repeat herself again, but he wanted to make sure that he got it. First of all, he thought that anyone coming here to take any of his people had a death wish, but then humans were stupid all the time.

"His name is Ramon Packer. His son is Ramon as well, but he's called Ramie." Shawn asked her why they were coming here. "To get me. They think that they can sell me off to the highest bidder and make a lot of money."

"But you can stop this?" Carmine told him that she could only delay it, not stop it. "So you want me to make this phone call, to slow this down."

"Yes, please." She was so polite. The conversation was about having someone arrested for murdering a woman, yet she was being as polite as if they were having tea. "Danielle is going to help the police find the gun, but the rest, calling in,

113

it has to come from you. You can say that one of your pack, it doesn't matter who, saw Ramie dispose of the gun in a wet concrete hole."

He looked at Quinn and the woman Danielle. He'd seen her around here before, but since he'd had no trouble from her, he'd not confronted her. He asked Quinn if she was all right with this.

"All right? No, I'm not all right. My sister is telling you how to slow down a man who is coming for her to kill her or sell her off, and there isn't a damned thing I can do about it. So, no, I'm not even close to being all right." He laughed and she glared at him. "I don't think you're funny either."

"No, ma'am, I'm not at all funny, but what I do find funny, and I'm sorry for it, is that in all my years, this is the very first time I've helped a dragon." She growled at him and Shawn laughed harder. "You're not helping me. Not one bit, my dear."

"The police need to be called now or the hole will be covered in concrete." He picked up the phone and made the call. "Don't forget, Mr. Shawn, your pack member saw it, not you."

He spoke to the person answering the phone, then was transferred to someone else when he told them what information he had. Glancing down at the newspaper, he wasn't at all surprised that Margie Shaw had been murdered. She was bad news, and had been for a good many years. She'd find herself a sucker, and a stupid one at that, and pull a scam on them. Sometimes she'd move out of town then come back when the pickings were ripe. This time she'd pulled her trick on the wrong man. Or one smarter than she'd thought. Telling the man on the phone what he had, he was put on hold once again and he looked at the young girl.

He'd heard about her. Danburn had come to him to ask if she could come to the school for a little while to be safe. Of course, he'd do anything for the dragon, include help watch over one of his flock. But when he'd told him what she could do, he'd been disbelieving at first, then he'd been astounded. Now she was sitting here in his office with not only her sister, but a vampire too.

"Shawn?" He sat up when he heard the voice of the chief of police, Marty Sherbet. "You sure you saw this kid dropping a gun down a hole?"

"Not me, but one of my pack. And they don't want you to know who it is. I think they might have some issues about police. But they said it was a pillar being poured, and that some of it had been poured a few days ago." He looked at Carmine when she gave him the thumbs up. "They said that they'd gone there today, and it looks like some more is going to be poured atop it. But he's sure there was a gun in there, and that Ramie Packer was the one that put it there."

"I sent two cars over there now, and I spoke to the foreman on the sight...he's going to hold off on things until we have a look." Shawn heard someone talking to Marty, then he spoke again. "Shawn, there's a gun there. The foreman called back... he said he took a flashlight and seen it there. We're going to send a car out to his house now."

"Weren't he and that Margie girl an item for a little while?" He told him that he'd been told the same thing. "I wonder what went down there. I don't know that one has to do with the other, but I figured with a gunshot to the head, that seems mighty peculiar."

After being thanked a few more times, he disconnected the call. Then he looked at the little girl. He had a lot of questions, and was sure that before he had answers to even half of them, he'd have that many more. But first things first, he asked about his pack.

"No one will be harmed at any time." He nodded. "So long as you do what I tell you. I don't mean that you have to jump rope or anything, but there are things that have to take place or he'll just come back or send someone else."

"And you know this." She glanced at Danielle, then back at him. Shawn asked the vampire what she knew. "I mean, you're here and not causing any trouble, so I have no beef with you. But why now? Why are you helping this child?"

"She's helping me. My father is coming after me, but I'll be safe here, so long as I too do what I am told. I have spoken to the dragon king, and he has given me safe passage. That will keep me safe for a very long time." He knew who her father was too, and her brother. Bad news there. "You will be safe as well. I will go against the council rules should you or yours look to be in trouble."

"You'll kill them." She nodded, then looked at Quinn when she said she'd do it. "I imagine that a dragon can do a great deal more harm to a vampire than another vampire. If you're smart, which you seem to be, then I'd let the dragons take care of him."

"Whatever it takes, it will be done so that no one is harmed, I promise."

Shawn started to tell her that he had his own magic, being as old as he was, but Quinn seemed to understand that. "I think, together, we can do a great deal of harm to him should it come to that. But for now, we're going to take care of this asshole that thinks taking my sister is going to be a piece of cake."

He laughed, he couldn't help it. To look at the three women, he'd bet that most would think that they were timid, sort of pushovers. But he knew better. The three of them, especially the older two, would kill anything that moved toward the little girl, and he hoped that he was around to see it. It was going to be epic. That was for sure.

After they left him, he called his pack leaders together and told them what was going to happen. Mostly it was about a man coming on the dragon's land and what they were to do about him, basically just let him know so that the dragons knew.

"Will he be a problem?" He told his second that he would, but not once he stepped out of line. "And we don't get to have any fun with him? Not even to play around a bit? It's been a little boring around here, sir. Could you ask for us?"

Picking up the phone, he called Danburn, but his lovely mother answered. When he told her what he knew and the questions that he had, she laughed too. He loved this woman, and had since he'd first met her all those centuries ago.

"A bit of fun shouldn't hurt anyone, I'd think. Let me clear it with the youngster. I say that like they're not all youngsters. Hang on, young man." He grinned at being called young anything, but he waited. "I've spoken to them, and they said that you could have your fun to scare him off should he arrive here before the twenty-second. That's a week and a half away. I'm sure that you can get into all sorts of mischief between now and then. Am I correct?"

"Yes, you are. And we'll not harm him, but just make him a little nervous. Thank you, my lady." She invited him to the house for Christmas, and he said he'd have to ask his wife. "She usually goes to her mother's for the holiday, but this year we've opted to stay here. The weather is brutal, but we love it for the snow. I'll ask her."

"See that you do. And we're going to have a nice gathering

in the glen come the day after Christmas for the young ones in the pack, as we usually do. I've gotten a count with ages from your wife, so we're set up." He thanked her again. "No problem, Shawn. You do so much for us that we love doing this for you and yours. Let us know if you need anything else."

Over the decades the English household had provided college educations to so many of his pack, as well as new baby items when a child was born, that he felt as if he'd do anything for them without hesitation. They never asked for more than they needed, and had not once brought up the gifts to the pack, but humbly asked for things that they needed.

Shawn looked up when his own wife came into the room with him. She had a look on her face, one that told him that she was upset. He'd bet anything that it was their youngest son. He'd been getting on her last nerve for the past two weeks. She had a fistful of receipts, and when she tossed them in his direction, he picked them up without looking at them. Andi would get to them.

"Did you know that there are any number of people in town that know our son? That they can pick them out of a long line that had many wolves in it?" Shawn nodded without agreeing or disagreeing. "Yet, when I told them, quite a few times, that they're not to extend credit to him, they tell me, his mother, that they didn't know it was him. How the hell was that to happen, I ask you?"

"Someone let him charge something?" She growled and he almost laughed. "Honey, I'm trying my best to understand what has you so upset."

"He charged nine hundred dollars to the local department store." He almost asked what the hell had cost nine hundred dollars, but she was on a roll. "A stereo. A stereo that I told

118

him he wasn't to have until he brought up his grades. So he went and bought it anyway."

He was in for it now. "I did that." She asked him what he'd done. "I bought the stereo the other day. It was on sale, and I knew that you were going to give it to him for Christmas, so I went ahead and purchased it. I forgot to tell you."

Andi sat there, her face red now that she was holding onto her anger. He started to tell her the price he'd gotten for it when she started laughing. Then, as she laughed more, holding her belly as she did so, he was worried that she'd gone off the deep end. Standing up to go to her, he was stopped when she started talking.

"I got it too." He frowned. "The other week, I was in the store and I saw that it was on sale. But since he was with me, I had your assistant go in and pay for it for me. Oh, Shawn, we're a pair, aren't we? We didn't save a lick of money because we now have two of them. We need to talk more, I think."

He started laughing too. It was funny. In order to save a few bucks, they'd spent twice that on something for a son that was as aggravating as they came. He got up and went to his wife to hold her. As soon as she was in his arms, he kissed her neck.

"I love you, Andi." She told him she loved him as well. "I guess we can find someone else that'll need a nice system. Maybe we can give it to the young dragon child. I heard that she is going to be adopted by the dragons."

"I talked to Lady Elissa and gave her the list she asked for." He said that he'd heard that too. "I was thinking that we should do something for the newest members. The mates to the other dragons. I think they'll all be moving here soon. I was thinking we could make them welcome packs."

"I don't think I know what that is." She grinned at him.

"Ah, you're making them welcome packs. All right, explain that to me so that I can approve it."

"We send two or three of the pack to them as a gift. They would work for them, helping our pack, and have an outside job instead of working around the camp. Some of them are wanting to leave...the younger pack members anyway. This way they can leave, but still be a part of this pack."

"Okay, but what if they don't want them to be hanging around the house? What kind of work do you think they'd be able to do?" She told him. "Okay, now that is a sellable point. Computer work around the house, the front gates of the houses. Which, I'm glad to say, they all have. Then I love your idea about them working within the house, as sitting for the babies when they come along. Have I told you lately how brilliant you are? You are, you know. As smart as, if not smarter than, most anyone I know."

He knew that they'd go for it. All of them would be very glad for the extra protection, as well as the help around the house. Big houses meant big problems if you didn't know the people working for you. Shawn told Andi that he'd talk to Danburn and the others tomorrow. She kissed him on the nose and left him. Shawn smiled. It was wonderful to have such a smart wife.

Chapter 9

Ramon stood at the front desk and waited until the man he'd been talking to got off the phone. He wasn't really sure what was going on, only that he'd been brought here, by the police, a couple of hours ago, then told to wait. And he'd been waiting for a long time. When the other man hung up the phone, he started again to ask him what he was there for when the phone rang. He was tempted to tell him to stop ignoring him when the chief came around the side of the desk and told him to come with him.

"Officer, was it necessary for me to be dragged down here in the middle of the morning? By a cruiser with the lights on too?" He said that it was. "Well, I don't know what for. I had a day planned out, and now I can't even get that done, I've been here so long."

"We arrested your son, Ramon Jr., this morning." He stopped walking and tried to breathe around his balls, which were suddenly up around his throat. The officer—Marty, he'd said his name was—turned and looked at him then, and waved him forward. "He's been arrested for murder, Ramon.

The murder of his girlfriend and lover, Margie Shaw."

"He killed her?" Ramon had practiced at home what he'd do if the police came for him. He had no idea if they would or not…no one seemed to care a fig that she was dead. So when the police showed up at his house, he'd not had a single clue that it was about Ramie. And now this. "When did you arrest him? You said this morning. I'm sorry, I'm having a hard time with this. I mean, he didn't do it. I'm sure of it."

"We found the gun. There was a witness to him tossing it in a pillar going up for the new school gym. Had we not heard from this person, then we might not have ever put him at the scene. The gun is a match for the one that killed her, and it's covered with his prints and her blood." Ramon nodded, not sure what to say now. His rehearsed lines hadn't gone this far. "He's asking for a lawyer, so we called you. He didn't want us to, said you had a job to do, but we figured you'd want to know."

"Yes, yes, of course. Thank you. Did he say what my job was? I mean, I didn't know that he knew I was working on something." Marty said only that he was working on something big. "I don't know if I'd call it big or not. It's just a job."

Ramon shut his mouth. He'd practiced that too, but so far he'd fucked that up. Don't say anything more than they ask you for, he'd told himself over and over. Yes, well, he'd not been doing such a good job on that one, had he? Then the other rule he'd tried drilling in his head was not to ask questions. So far, he thought, he'd asked a dozen or more of them.

"He knows that you're here, but I don't know if he'll see you or not. But as I said, he needs an attorney, and soon." Ramon said he wasn't sure how much he could afford. "Well,

I'd just let him take a court appointed one then. He's a grown man, Ramon, and they'll take care of it. I have to tell you something…we want him to confess. If he does, it might go easier on him. I was hoping you could have a word or two with him."

"You mean tell him to confess? I don't know. That's admitting that he's done it, isn't it? I mean, how do you know he was even near her when she was shot? Anyone could have seen her coming out of that building." Marty looked at him oddly, but didn't comment. He wanted to ask what he'd said wrong, but he closed his mouth so tightly that he hurt his tongue.

"You talk to him for me."

He said that he would. As he was led into a little room, he felt like there were ten thousand eyes on him. The big mirror was, in his mind, a large television screen that was taping his every move. Or perhaps it was monitoring his body temperature, like in those shows where it told you were lying or something. The air conditioning vents were hidden microphones recording his every breath, as well as holding everything he said against him. He stretched his collar out and then clasped his hands in front of him. He knew he was giving away everything with body tells, like he was one of those high stake poker players giving it all away by a single movement.

Ramon was left in the little room and told to wait. For what, he wasn't sure. To confess that he knew? Maybe they wanted him to say that he'd helped his son? Whatever it was, he wasn't having any of it. Ramie had done this. Of course, he had given him money, and a credit card, as well as a phone. Ramon supposed he was in as deep as his son was on this.

His son was brought in, and he could tell right away that

he'd been crying. The moron was going to get himself raped if he didn't stop acting like a little girl. As soon as he sat down across from him and his hands were cuffed to the table, he wanted to ask him what he'd told anyone. But, true to form, his son started talking all on his own.

"They want me to confess to it. They only got the gun. I'm not sure how they found it, Dad. I put it in there, and it should have had more concrete poured over it by now." He told his son that they were being recorded. "They can't do that. I didn't say they could. That's against the law."

"So is murder, but that's what they got you in here for, isn't it?" Ramie nodded and started crying again. "Sit up and shut your mouth. What the hell were you thinking? You weren't, that's what is going on. They want you to confess to killing her so that they can try to get you a lesser sentence. Did you kill her?"

He knew that Ramie was going to say that he had known, that he knew he'd even given him money to run. But all he did was nod, then look at him. It was the first time in a very long time that he wanted to hold his little boy. Comfort him and tell him that things would be all right. But it wouldn't. Not now, not ever again.

"Tell them what they need to know, Ramie. That way when it goes to court, then you can plead down." He asked him if he'd stay with him while he did it. "I can do that. You just tell them what happened and why you did it."

"All right, Dad." The police officer that was in the room with them went to get someone. Another person came in the room, so there was no chance for him to speak to Ramie alone. There was so much he wanted to ask him, so many things he wanted to tell him, but not now. Not in here.

The attorney had to be present when he made his

confession. Also, the person that did the recording of the event was out on sick leave and would be back soon, and they'd call him when he was there. Could he please return then? He looked at his son and wanted to tell him that he had plans too, but decided a little more time wasn't going to make a difference, so he agreed.

The getting of this kid was stretching out more and more all the time. It was as if someone was working against him in this. He had a fleeting thought that the kid might be doing it, but didn't think that was right. She might know how to do a lot of things, but he doubted very much she would know that he was coming for her. And when.

After getting the time straight, he said that he'd return in the morning. Ramie could have some books to read and some snacks, but nothing else. Ramon knew that the only books that his son read were girly magazines, and his snacks tended to be things like steak and a baked potato. Ramie had never been a chip or cookie eater, more of a meal every couple of hours eater.

Going home, he was disappointed to find out that it was too late for him to go to the school to check things out. The gates were locked up, and the only way he'd found to get on the property was to crawl over a five foot fence, then go through a grove of trees and hope he didn't get lost in the swamp that seemed to be all around the place. He'd go in the early morning, before going to the jail. Christ, this was getting to be an all week project, when it should have only been a snatch and go thing.

When he woke the next morning, it was still dark out. Just the way he wanted it to be. As he dressed in his darkest clothing, he laid out his clothes that he was going to wear to the jail to see his son. As he was leaving, he went back in the house for his flashlight, as well as his pocket knife. He didn't want to be caught with nothing on him in the event that he ran into something or someone.

Ramon parked as close as he could to the fence and got out. Seeing a movement out of the corner of his eye made him pause, but the harder he stared, the more he thought it was just the wind. Climbing over the fence, he was about halfway to the trees on the other side when he thought he might make it all the way.

He was feeling pretty good about things. If this worked out, he told himself, then his son should be just fine too. They'd sell off the kid, then the two of them would run off. Go to another country and live the good life. It was a solid plan, he thought.

Something hit him from behind just as the building came into view. Ramon was sure that it was something big, but for the life of him, he couldn't see a damned thing when he sat up to look around. When he was starting to stand up, he felt something hit him again, this time knocking him head over ass until he thought he was turned around. Sitting as still as he could, he looked around. That was when he saw them.

There were eyes glowing back at him. His flashlight caught them several times when he searched, but he couldn't see what they were. He was suddenly afraid. Whatever was out there, they were big, and there were a lot of them. Standing up, he nervously called out.

"I have a gun." He pretended to hold one in his pocket. "Whoever you are, you should know that I'm a crack shot."

The low growl had him turning in a circle too quickly. Of course, since he was already nervous and scared, he fell again. This time when he started to stand up, something—a big fucking something—stood on his back. The bite of something

126

sharp dug into his backside until he cried out in pain.

"Who's there?" The growl again came from his back, but he couldn't turn to see. "Let me up."

This time the smell of blood touched his nose. It was strong, and made him think that he was going to lose his urine. When the thing at his back moved off him, Ramon got a good look at the beast that had knocked him to the ground.

A wolf. A large, sharp toothed wolf that looked like it could swallow him down in one bite. When he started to move, to sit up then run, several more wolves came out of the woods and stared at him, their hackles high on their backs and their teeth almost glowing in the dawning sunlight.

To him it looked as if they had blood dripping from their canines. Of course it wasn't...at least he tried to tell himself that it wasn't. But they were fucking huge, like they'd been fed some kind of drugs that had him thinking they were ten times...no, twenty times bigger than the normal wolf. And meaner looking too.

There were at least two dozen of them, circled around him like they were going to attack at any moment. He was pretty sure that they were, and he wanted to beg for his life. Standing up, careful where he stepped, he backed up, but then hit the tree behind him.

He was sure that they were laughing at him. When he hit the big tree, he'd cried out like a child, screaming like he'd been bitten by a large snake. Or a wolf. Backing up more, he kept telling the beasts that he was leaving, that he'd come back when they were less busy. Just as he was thinking he was going to make it, one of them, the largest of them, walked up to him and peed on him.

It was on the tip of his tongue to scream at the thing, to take out his knife and show it who he was messing with. He

127

wanted to tell him that wasn't right. But at the last moment, he remembered the teeth and the size of the monster. Backing up again, he watched as they peeled away from the larger one, one by one, until it was just him. Then he was no longer a wolf, but a man. A very large and scary one at that.

"You'll leave here and not return." The man standing before him startled him enough that Ramon fell to the ground. The wolf, it seemed to him, had just disappeared, and the man took his place. "If you return my pack will kill you."

"All right." Ramon waited for the man to say more, anything, but when he lifted his head to talk to him, the man and the pack of wolves were gone. Just as if they'd never been there. Ramon was sure that he'd dreamed the entire thing and felt his bravery return. "I'll come back when I want. No stupid dog is going to tell me what to do. You can't make me do a damned thing."

Brave words he knew, now that he was alone, but he was feeling dumber with each step he took back to his car. And when he got there, his doors were opened and the clothing that he was to wear to the jail was lying in a heap of dog shit. More than likely wolf shit. Cursing about the extra time he'd have to take to go home, his alarm went off and he knew that he was going to be the laughingstock of the jail. He was going there with the wolf pee all over him, along with the mud and other nastiness he'd picked up when he'd fallen.

~~~

Hanson laughed every time he thought of Ramon getting his ass handed to him by the pack. Shawn told him that he'd regretted that they'd only played with him a little, but that when he came back, they were going to let him get a little closer to the buildings before they came after him.

"Andi was with us or I might have bitten him a little, but

she said that if I did that, he might not return at all. And I have to tell you, Hanson, it was a blast that I'd like to be in on a few more times." Hanson said for him to have fun. "We are. Thank you. By the way, have you spoken to Danburn about the pack welcoming committee? Andi thinks it will keep the younger wolves around longer."

"I know that he was very happy with the idea. I am as well. Having the extra people around, especially right now, is welcome." Shawn nodded. "I've been meaning to ask you something for a couple of days now. Do you know if there is any land for sale? I'm looking to bring some of my businesses here, and that would help me and you in the long run."

"Yes. There are about six hundred acres not far from your house." He told him where it was. "What sort of business are you thinking about? Some that will hire some lonely wolf pack? While we're doing well right now, the leaner months of winter are when we suffer the most. It's not like it used to be around here. No real businesses that can keep the money flowing."

"Yes. As a matter of fact, that is something else that I needed to talk to you about. My wife is wanting to open a diner, home cooking, and she'll need some workers. And my business will need to hire not just construction workers to build, but workers too. It's a distribution plant. We made plastics for cell phone shells. Also, we just signed a contract to make them for a large dealer in phones. It'll be good for this area, I believe."

"I love both of those ideas. And a diner would be wonderful around here. The only restaurants that we have right now are a burger place that is good, but no fine dining, and a restaurant that serves things that most of us won't touch." Hanson asked him what they served. "Little bitty bits of food on a large plate that has so much sauce around it, it looks like a mess. And it costs more than most of the people make in a week. Too expensive."

"Quinn wants to make comfort food. And I have to tell you, Shawn, if she cooks like she does at the house, then we'll all need to have bigger clothing. It's that good. And her apple raspberry pie is so delicious, it makes a man want to beg for a second helping." Shawn said he loved pie. "Then you help me convince her that she needs to do this. For all mankind. Come to dinner tonight with the missus, and we'll have a good meal and you can convince her."

"You're throwing your old friend under the bus, are you?" Hanson nodded. "You old devil you. All right, I'll do it, but you'll owe me if it's not as good as you say. Not that I don't believe you, but some man's good food isn't another's."

He was still grinning when Shawn left. Hanson went to find Quinn to tell her they were having company for dinner, and found her in the kitchen with the other two women of their little pack. They seemed to be tasting everything that Quinn was cooking. As soon as they spotted him, he was dragged into the conversation about opening a restaurant of her own.

"I've been trying to tell her that for weeks now." He took one of the offered scones and ate it while he continued. "She makes this tart pie that melts in your mouth. And the pot roast we had last night was so tender and juicy that I swear, the gravy we had with it seemed to make it like heaven. And her green beans...my goodness, you should have—"

"Okay, we're coming for dinner tonight." Kendrick laughed and smacked him on the hand when he reached for the last scone that looked like blueberry. "And this is all your fault. We should have just quit at desserts, but now we'll have to have it all. And as for the diner? You'll open it for no other reason than we'll have someplace to go eat with you. This is amazing."

When the women left, he told her that Shawn and Andi were coming as well. She just nodded and continued to clean up the flour that she'd been using to make homemade bread. He was concerned because she didn't give him a hard time, nor did she try and talk him out of the diner.

"I spoke to Carmine today. She thinks that the men are after her because Mom called them." He leaned back in his chair and asked her what she thought. "I don't know. So far everything that she's said has come true. But Carmine said that Mom didn't turn her in, but had called for information about her. And that is what got them looking for her. I'm concerned at how many other people she talked to."

"What does Carmine say?" She shrugged. "That's not an answer, honey. Did she think your mom called anyone else or not?"

"She said that Mom called this company that dealt with government weaponry. Why would she do that?" Quinn sat down across from him, handing him another scone. "I mean, why didn't she call the hospital, or even a doctor? Why the government?"

"I don't know. I mean, without her being here to ask, then we might not ever know. But Carmine seems to think that dealing with this other man, it'll end with him. Do you trust her?" She said she wasn't sure how to have confidence in anyone anymore. "I'm sorry about that. I am. But if she said he'd be it, then I'd believe her. If it makes you feel any better, Ramon did show up today on the property and was chased away by the wolf pack."

"She said that he'd be here." Quinn got up and pulled

things from the cabinets. He went to her and held her to him when she put everything down. "I'm so afraid for her. I don't understand most of the things she can do, but she's my sister and I'm terrified for her."

"I know that. And we'll all take care that she's safe." Hanson explained about the extra patrols around the place, as well as the men he'd hired to come in and watch over her and the others until this was done. "We're doing everything we can here, and I think, what with us all being dragons, that things will be a lot better than had we just been humans."

"Kendrick and I were in the yard earlier messing with our dragons. It's easier when there aren't a lot of people around, I think. We're still having trouble flying...not so much the taking off, but the landing is a little difficult to get used to." He told her that it would come to them. "I hope so. Also, we went to the lake around their home. Did you know that it's deeper than it looks? I mean, like leagues deeper. Anyway, when we came out of the water as our dragons, our scales fell off into it, and Noah told us that it was repayment for eating the fish. I didn't realize that we'd done all that much, eating I mean, but the dragons seemed to know to do it."

"Yes. When my dragon is hungry, it's strange. I can be so full, like after one of your meals, that I feel like I'm going to burst. But the dragon, he is starving, and will kill a lake in no time. Leaving behind the magic of the scales, it repays, as Noah said, the waterway with magic so that they can have more fish." She pulled away and started putting things together in a large bowl. "I've spoken to Dana and Griffith. We're going to try our best to bring some work to the area. I have Shawn looking for some land that we can use for building. And Kip has several construction businesses that he said he could help out with as well. Hire some of the locals."

"And then there is the diner that you think I should open." He grinned at her. "Andi called me an hour ago, while the other two were here, and told me that she had the perfect place for it. Imagine my surprise when she said that you'd convinced Shawn that I'd need cooks and whatnot to get it running."

"Are you mad?" She said that she wasn't, not really. "Great. I'm thinking after tonight, with everyone here, you're going to not just be begged to open it, but they're going to pledge you money and also a lot of support. It's going to be great. Not just for you, but the community as well."

"Sure, easy for you to say. Also, I have a name to call it. Carmine came in earlier and told me that I should name it Dragon's Lair. I have no idea why, but she said that it had a nice ring to it. I asked her if dragons had a lair, and she assured me that they did. And that I needed a magnificent dragon that spewed heat from its mouth. I think that's a little over the top, but she only laughed."

When he left her, she'd not only gotten the bread into loaf pans, but she'd put on several cans of green beans and had cut up some chickens. Her fried chicken was the best he'd ever eaten, and he wasn't sure now that anyone should come to dinner. He wanted leftovers. Oh well, he thought, sharing once wasn't going to kill him, and he rubbed his growling belly.

Chapter 10

Ramon was at the police station early the next morning. He had a plan to get to the girl, and it was going to require him to be out all night. He wasn't sure how well that was going to work, but he'd gotten a gun and a tent. His thinking was that he'd spend the night in the tent, they'd leave him be, and he'd nab the girl first thing, before the monsters were out of bed, and then he'd be set up.

"I'll show them, now won't I?" He looked at the man next to him when he asked him what he was saying. "Mind your own business. I'm not talking to you."

When the man got up and left him there, he thought about yesterday morning instead of the odd looks he'd gotten from the people in the station. He'd tried again to get on the property, and had been almost to the building when he'd seen the pack again. He'd never run so fast in his life to get away from them. But they still managed not only to pee on him again, this time his back and head, but had torn his clothing. Ramon had had to go home after that and shower and change. It was nasty, the way wolf piss felt on his body. And he'd had to burn his clothing too. No wearing it again.

Then last night he'd been by the fence and had watched for an hour to see if they were out and about at night. The early morning had been the only time he'd been there up until now, and he figured out that they weren't out at all during the nighttime. So with that bit of information, he was going to go in at night, tonight as a matter of fact, and then sneak his way to the school as soon as the sun was up enough for him to see. He had to get that girl. His buyer was getting mighty antsy. Not to mention, Ramon didn't think he believed that she was real anymore.

"She is, you can trust me on this." The man, McDonald, like that fucking farmer, had told him that the proof was in the pudding. Whatever the hell that was supposed to mean. "She can do all kinds of shit with her mind. Like, I think she's been messing with me the whole time I've been trying to kidnap her."

"Kidnap her? You told me that you had it in the bag. I'm even surer that you told me that you were good friends with her family, and that she was willing to come around to meet me. I don't condone kidnapping. Not one bit." He told McDonald that he was friends, he just needed to work out the details when he spoke again. "You bring her to me in the next forty-eight hours, and she'd better be willing and we'll talk. But no more kidnapping."

He had about twenty-four hours left of the forty-eight, and still no girl. But he had a plan, and the plan was to get her in the morning, then take her to see this bozo and get paid. Ramon had no idea what to do to help his son, and reckoned that he'd just have to figure things out on his own. As soon as this confession shit was over with, anyway.

"Mr. Packer, we can take you back now." He stood up

and made his way to the same room he'd been in before. "We have it all set up now, and everyone is in place except for Ramie. We'll get him as soon as you're seated."

Nodding, he thought of his lines. He's not just practiced them in front of the mirror all day yesterday, but he'd also written them down, over and over, like he'd had to do in grade school when he'd miss a spelling word. The two men that were already in the room introduced themselves to him. One was Ramie's court appointed attorney, and the other was the witness to what was going to go on today. Seemed like overkill to him, what with them recording it on a tape player and the camera on a pole in the corner. But he wasn't in charge of things like this, and supposed this was how they did it. There were also two officers there that said nothing.

When Ramie was brought in, Ramon looked at his son. He had a black eye and a busted lip. There were cuts on his chin, as well as his forehead. Ramon wanted to ask what the fuck had happened, but the attorney, whatever his name had been, answered first.

"Mr. Packer met with an accident in the men's room last night." Ramon asked the officer if he'd been raped. "Not that he said. He did say that he fell twice before he had his footing under him."

"I don't want to talk about it." Ramie looked at him. "Dad, you have to get me out of here. These people are treating me really bad. I don't want to be here."

"Of course you don't, son. But you have to own up to what you did, now don't you?" Ramie nodded and dropped his head. "All right now, you talk to these men about what happened. All right?"

Ramie started talking about how he'd been dating Margie for the last several months. Then she'd moved closer to him by finding her a place in town and it got serious. Mostly since the spring, but off and on because they'd have a row and break up for a little while. Not too long, but a couple of days at a time, he guessed. When he was talking about how much he'd loved her and trusted her, Ramon zoned out. He needed to get his plan right in his head for tonight.

He had to pick up some water and a few snacks. After that he was going to hike as far as he could to the school, and hide in the tent for the rest of the night. Ramon thought about having to pee and such, and decided that he could hold it, that he'd just wait until morning to get out of the tent to relieve himself. If worse come to worst, he thought, he'd just pee in one of the bottles of water he was taking after it was empty.

"Dad?" He looked around the room and everyone was staring at him. He didn't have a clue what was going on, and was afraid that he'd missed something very important. "They asked you about the phone you gave me."

"I was always giving you a phone, Ramie. I had to go to those burner kind because you was using up all my data." Good, he thought that was one of the things he'd practiced. "You kept losing the expensive ones, right?"

"But you gave me one the morning I told you about Margie." He felt like he was trapped; his breathing, as well as his heart, had been backed up in his chest. When Ramon shook his head, Ramie nodded. "You did. Along with the money you had in your pocket. Remember?"

"Ramie, I think you're confused about some other time. I didn't give you anything." Ramon looked around the room. "You know how kids are. They're forever with their hands out. He's just confused."

Ramon was afraid when they seemed to pause in their

waiting on Ramie to continue. Even the fan that was running appeared to have taken a breather. Sitting as still as he could, knowing that squirming would give him away, he waited. And in a few moments, which to him seemed like hours, the officer asked Ramie to go on about meeting Margie.

"She told me that she was going to have a baby, and that it was mine. Dad told me that it was a lie, and when she told me that she needed money for the baby furniture that she ordered, Dad told me that he wasn't paying for it. And that I should go to the doctors with her." The officer asked him if he'd gone. "No. She wouldn't let me. Told me that it was a girl thing, and that she'd call me to pick her up afterwards. But I followed her."

"Did you go there with the intent to kill her?" Ramie said that he'd not. "Did your dad tell you to kill her?" Ramon started to object, but was stopped by the other officer who held him down.

"No. Dad only said that I should go with her. That he thought she was a little too old to be having a kid anyway. I don't know how he knew, but he was right. And when she went to the gambling place out on Tenth, I knew I was being had. Just like my dad told me. And they knew her there too. I guess she'd been going there for a long time, huh?" The officer asked him where he'd gotten the car. "I borrowed it. I didn't want her to know that I was following her, so I went to the market out where I used to work and borrowed one. I took it right back when I was…when I was done."

"You stole a car to go and kill your girlfriend." Ramie said that he'd not. That he'd only wanted to follow her without her knowledge. "So where did you get the gun?"

"I was looking for a piece of paper to put on the door. You know, telling her that I knew she was lying and all, but

I found the gun. And before I knew what I'd done, she was dead." He looked at Ramon, then dropped his head again. "I was in love with her. I was. But she lied to me. About a lot of things."

They asked him a few more questions, mostly about the gun and car, then about the baby. It seemed to Ramon that they were asking him the same questions over and over, only twisting them up a bit, but Ramie never changed his story. When they were done, Ramon was asked to wait while they took Ramie back to his cell.

Ramon knew they were going to ask him about his part in his son running off like he had. But when they returned a few minutes later, the attorney said that he'd be in touch with him when he was finished and he was released. It seemed to Ramon that he was being shoved out the door before he could think that they weren't asking him about anything his son had said. As he made his way to the car, he hurried along, terrified that they were going to change their mind and call him back in.

He was at the store, picking up the things he might need for tonight, when he realized how easily he'd gotten off. Ramie was going to prison, that much he was sure of. For how long was anyone's guess. And he'd not have to share the money, any of it, with anyone but himself. Ramon felt a little lighter as he paid for his water and jerky and headed to his car.

"This is gonna work." He barely caught himself from dancing around his car before he got into it. The tent was in the back seat, the water was deep in the cooler that he'd bought, and it was iced down. There was a thick sleeping bag that he'd gotten, as well as a blow up pillow to sleep on and a change of clothing. Ramon was quite pleased with himself as he drove to the fence line again.

He didn't see a single wolf as he made his way to the school. He'd been there so many times that he knew the route by heart now. But he was only a few yards away from it when he started to feel like he wasn't going to make it physically. Everything that he had on him seemed to double in weight with each step he took.

The cooler was too heavy for him to drag it by the wheels, and it kept getting stuck in the grass and dead leaves. The backpack that held everything he thought he'd need for a night was digging painfully into his back, and he nearly fell over when he bent to pick up the cooler to carry. By the time he'd gone a few more yards, he had a feeling that he should have thought this out a little more. Panting and sweating like a pig, he had to rest more and more as he walked with his load.

Turning, he saw that he'd not even gone far enough yet to not see his car. Christ, he was going to be dead, or too tired to grab the girl at this rate. Things never worked out just the way you thought they should in your head, he thought. And he'd assumed that he'd worked this right to the bone.

When he'd gone about as far as he could, he pulled out his tent and the other things he'd brought. The tent, still in the package, had instructions, but they were in another language. He wasn't even sure what it was. There were pictures too, but as dark as it was in the woods, it was difficult to tell if he was reading them right or not. Ramon wasn't going to let a tent get the better of him, so he laid out all the pieces and started again.

The rain started about ten minutes into his trying to put his tent up the fourth time. As the rain started to pour, making puddles in his tent before he could get it to stand, Ramon started cursing. It was that or throw the poles as far as he could. And they were long too, about fourteen feet, he'd bet. But he was determined, damn it, to get it set up, no matter what adversities came his way. Suddenly the night sky lit up and the lightning streaked across the sky like it was searching for his body to zap.

~~~

"Then he pulls out this long pole and looks at it as if it's going to all of a sudden tell him how to put it together. I swear to you, Hanson, it was like watching a comedy of errors as he stood there working to get the things set up. And he never did figure it out. I would have stayed there in the rain all night, if I could have." Hanson asked him what they'd done then. "Nothing. Didn't really seem to be any point. He was doing a fine job of it on his own. I guess we could have helped him along—you know, given him the instructions in English—but I don't know that it would have done him any good. And after he threw the poles, water bottles, and all into the woods and stomped off, we just waited until he was gone and cleaned up the mess. My son is going to keep the tent, which he put together without any trouble. He's going to use it on trips in the summer with his friends."

"Ramon Packer is a moron." Shawn agreed with him. "We have to get things moving on this end with Carmine. I don't know what she knows, but she's been very quiet lately. I think it's the new school, but at this point, I don't know what to expect. But I thank you for your help. It's good to know you had such a good time too."

"It was a lot of fun. The most I've had in a long time." Shawn stood up and stretched, laughing as he continued. "Well, anyway, he's back at his house, fuming from what I could hear when he went inside. But we have people on him, and as soon as he leaves again, we'll let you know."

"Thanks." He said it was his pleasure. "Also, the building that your wife told Quinn about is perfect. Quinn was so excited about it that I was sure she wanted to start renovating right then. And your guys are perfect for the jobs we have for them to get the structure up and going. I'm sure that this time next year we'll not only have a business up, but working too. It's going to help a lot of people, and me."

When Shawn left him to his work, Hanson thought of all the things that were going on right now. There was the new building going to be built. The school was getting some improvements that had been a long time in getting done. As far as he could see, Rett was doing an amazing job as mayor, and thought he'd be a shoe in next election. Hanson was putting the final touches on a couple of more projects he had going when he looked up and saw Carmine had joined him sometime in his work.

"You were busy, so I didn't want to bother you until you were finished." He said he was never too busy for her. "I have to ask you something. It's not bad, but I don't know how it works. Can you help me?"

"Sure. And if I don't know, then I can find you someone that does." She said that he'd know. "Okay. Ask away."

"Danielle is a vampire and a friend of mine. I wanted to ask you how it is that she can go out into the sunlight some days, and other days it's too much for her. I thought about asking her, but she so nervous when someone asks her about being a vampire." He nodded, understanding more than Carmine ever could about her friend. "Also, what happens to her if she were to drink from a dragon? I mean, if she could."

"Okay. But if I tell you more than you want to know, I'll stop." She nodded. "She can tolerate the sun more when she's fed well. She's old, several hundred years old, and doesn't

143

need as much as a younger vampire might need to stay alive. Not to mention, she's a full blooded vampire. There aren't that many of her kind left, having bred themselves with other creatures and humans. Anyway, being what she is, and with her age, she can tolerate more, as I said, and after feeding, she can stand a good deal more."

"So, if she'd had a nice dinner or whatever, she can do more than she could if she was hungry." Hanson said that was right. "And the dragon blood? What can that do for her?"

"She can't drink from a dragon. If she were mated to one she could enjoy a taste or two, but she cannot feed fully from a dragon. It would kill her." Carmine asked why. "Our blood, it…. Dragon blood is very strong. Magical too. And only a few, very few, know the value, both medically as well as magically, of what it can do to someone. For instance, it'll make someone immortal with just a sip. There is also the other parts of a dragon, all magical, that cannot just bring a lot of money should someone take them, but also be used for all manner of things. Scales can make a female ripe for pregnancy. The meat of a dragon has powers to bring back the dead, but that isn't well known. Also, there are things in our nails, when used properly, that can render a person seemingly dead to anyone who were to test them. So, since vampire blood is also very magical, the combination of the two would be toxic to the vampire. To us as well should we consume a great deal of it, but that would be more than she has in her body. In fact, several hundred vampires wouldn't bother us so much because of our size. Does that make sense?"

"Yes, it does." He asked her why she'd asked. "Because I want her to be stronger when her family comes here. I don't think they will, not for a while anyway, but she needs everything she can use against them. Her dad isn't a nice person. He wants her to marry so that he can control her through her mate."

"I see. And she knows this?" Carmine said that she did. "We can help her with that. All she has to do is pledge herself to one of us. Or you. You're a daughter of a very powerful dragon, and that would be me, honey. And with her pledge to keep you safe from all harm, then we would accept her as our own as well."

"And that's all it'll take? For her not to have to do what he tells her?" Hanson told her it was a little more than that, rules that she'd have to abide by, but pretty much. "How do I find the rules for her? So she can be my friend?"

"She knows the rules, Carmine. And the consequences should she break them." Carmine didn't say anything, but he could almost hear her mind working over that information. "Ask her about them. They're pretty straight forward, but should she break even one of them, then she's dead. I mean, with a dragon pledge, she'd die the moment that she broke it...there would be no second chances with it."

"Okay, I'll talk to her." She stood up and was about to the door when she looked back at him. He almost asked her not to speak. He had a feeling that whatever she said, it was going to be something bad. "When that man comes here, killing him is the only way to end this thing with him. And you have to do it. Quinn will want to, but you can't let her. If she does, then it'll hurt her in her heart."

"I'll do it. Anything to protect you." She smiled and then left the room. Almost as soon as she was gone, his phone rang. It was Shawn. "What can I do for you?"

"Ramie Packer was found dead in his cell this morning. He'd hung himself. He left a note, written on toilet paper, saying that he had killed the only woman he'd loved, and he just couldn't stand to live anymore." Hanson asked him what the police were saying. "Not much of anything right now. I don't think they expected it. I mean, he'd been beaten up a couple of times by another inmate because they thought him a sissy, but that's about it. From what I've heard, he would cry himself to sleep every night, then in the daylight hours, he'd sit on his bed wailing about how he'd killed her. Not very many want to hear that all the time, I guess."

"Does his dad know?" Shawn said that he didn't think so. He'd only found out because one of his pack worked in there. "Let me know what you find out. It's a shame, really, that it had to end this way, but he would never have made it in prison, not the way he was acting."

After putting the phone down, he decided to go and find Quinn. He needed some down time, some time for them to be together. Quinn was putting together a menu for the week to get the grocery list made from it when he asked her if she wanted to go flying with him. When she agreed so readily, he knew this was a good thing. As soon as they were ready to go, they headed to the yard. This was a much needed relief from all the stress they'd been under lately.

The snow was just beginning to come down when he took his dragon form. His dragon seemed to think it was time to go, and took off toward the darkening clouds almost immediately. When Quinn joined him as her own dragon, he laughed. The sky was dark enough to hide them, yet bright enough that he could see her dragon well.

I needed this. Thank you. He said it was his pleasure. *Does your dragon talk to you? I mean, like it's a whole other person? Mine does. She talks to me about what she wants to do, like fly and to be free.*

I don't think that she was happy with my parents. And to

146

be honest with you, I'd never heard of a dragon being taken from another person and given to someone else until I found out from Elissa. I just thought the earth would take her. She said that she told her that too. *What else?*

That she was happy that she'd come to me. By the way, I had no idea, but a dragon has no gender until it is paired with a holder. That's why Kendrick's dragon is a female as well. He'd not known that either. *Anyway, she told me that she is happy to be with us, that she's sorry that your parents are both gone, but they were not nice people. She also said that your sister's dragon is waiting too.*

He nearly fell to the earth. His entire being felt as if it had been given a deadly blow. Landing atop the mountain, he waited for her to land with him before he spoke. Hanson wasn't sure how his sister's dragon was still around, but knew that his dragon knew it as well.

She is alone, lonely too. Hanson asked if she asked after him. *Oh yes. She sees you when you think of her. But she would like for you to let her choose a person to be a part of.*

Does she have someone in mind? Quinn nodded, and said he did as well. *Yes, I suppose I do. When will she move? Do you know?*

No, I'm sorry. I'm not sure that she knows either. I think that the timing has to be right. Not just for her, but for the other half of her as well. Who did you think about when I asked you? He told her. *Yes, I thought you might say that. Rett will be good for them both. And if he's a dragon, he'll be safer as well, don't you think?*

Yes. He's a good man. And it would be wonderful knowing that my sister's dragon, however that works, would have a man like him taking her over. Quinn became a woman, but he wasn't ready to join her just yet and laid down. She leaned against him, her body in the crook of his arm. *I spoke to Carmine today. She came to my office.*

147

"She told me. Carmine was excited that you told her that you'd do anything for her. And happy that you told her that she was the daughter of a powerful dragon. Thank you for that." He said that she was his daughter until she told him she wanted something else. "I'm going to adopt her. Once we're married, I'm going to petition to the courts for her to be my daughter. I think we'll still think of each other as sisters, but it'll be easier on both of us if we have the courts make it legal."

We'll both adopt her then. That way she'll truly be my daughter, and she'll carry our last name as well. I think that'll be better for all of us.

When she stretched out, he felt her body relax by degrees. It was an amazing feeling, to be so large and have someone so small trust him like this. As he laid there with her, protecting her both from the world and the elements, Hanson thought he could spend the remainder of his days right here with her in his arms.

Chapter 11

Quinn moved around the building's first floor. There really wasn't much to see, very little as a matter of fact, but she was trying her best not to beg someone to start working on it as she told them what she wanted. Instead, she made notes. Like which walls needed to be brought down, and where she wanted the counter and kitchen things. This was much like being let loose in a candy store for some, she thought. When she heard someone laugh, she turned to look at Elissa. The woman was sitting on a dirty chair when Quinn joined her.

"I take it you're not very patient with this." Quinn said that she normally was, but not with this. "Have a seat, dear. I've been shopping all day with your sister, who I adore by the way, and my feet aren't doing as well as I would have hoped. My goodness, where does she get her energy?"

"I don't know. I'd like to have a bit of it now and again. Thank you for taking her. She was so excited to have a grandma taking her. I hope she didn't wear you out too much, or make you buy her everything in the place." Elissa just waved her off. "She's not had a great deal of things in her life. My mom

149

was so ill toward the end, and there wasn't much in the way of money to get things that she wanted, much less needed. I'm afraid that Carmine had to do without a great deal."

"Yes, and I would imagine that you did as well." Quinn said nothing. "I wanted to talk to you about the holidays. Christmas is in a few short weeks, and I was wondering what you might think about having everyone over to your home for breakfast. Then later in the day we could go to the castle for dinner. I've spoken to Kendrick about it, and she asked me to see what you think. I've also talked to Cassie, who I have to say is less than helpful about arrangements. Poor thing, I think she's overwhelmed by all this. Not us, but what we do when we're together."

"She's not had a good time of it either, I don't think." Elissa said that she hadn't and left it at that. "I can do whatever you wish. In fact, I'm actually thinking about having a few trial dinners with all of you before I get this place up and running. Everyone is so nice about my cooking, and I'm afraid that they're only being nice because I'm this bad assed dragon."

"Oh my. Yes, I can see that. But trust me when I tell you, child, it's just as wonderful as, if not better than, they're telling you. I've had some amazing meals in my time, even abroad. But your cooking is absolutely divine." Quinn thanked her. "No need for that. I'm telling you the truth. Also, I've wanted to talk to you about some cakes that we auction off a couple of days before Christmas. The money goes for a good cause. It helps some of the people around here with winter bills and food when they need it. We have the auction just before Christmas, and that money goes for the next year. Sometimes we run short, but Danburn usually makes up for it."

"I'd love to help out. I love to bake, and again this will be the perfect time for me to get some idea what sort of things people will like." As they sat there talking about what kinds of pies and cakes to bake, she saw a man wandering up and down the street in front of the building. She knew that she wasn't as attentive as she should have been, and when Elissa asked her what she saw, she turned to look as well. "I've seen him before. I don't know where, but he's been around a few times in the last several days."

"His name is DuPont. I believe his first name is David, but I can't be sure. He usually goes by Du for some reason. Anyway, he's homeless, but doesn't like to go to the shelter, even when it's very cold." She asked what he used to do for a living. "I'm not sure. He will tell you different stories each time you speak to him. He's been a teacher. A priest. Once he told me that he was a doctor. I'm not sure which to believe, or if I should believe any of them. But he's a kind old man."

"You think he'd come in and talk to me?" Elissa said that he would but asked her why. "I don't know, but I think I could use him for a couple of things. I believe he needs me."

Before Quinn could change her mind, she went to the door and waited for him to go past again before speaking. He was talking, she thought to himself, but she didn't know for sure. As he made his way to her again, she smiled at him and he stopped walking and spoke. Quinn told him her name, as well as the fact that she was going to open a place to get food soon.

"Could have used a good meal or two in my time. Mostly of late. I'm Du. That's what they call me. But you can call me Davie if you want." She told him that she'd like that. "You're that girl, the one that is mated to Hanson. You got that little girl what's been in town. She's smart as a tack, ain't she?"

"She is. And she's my sister, Carmine." He nodded. "Davie, there are people looking for her, did you know that?"

151

"Seen them. One anyway. He's been around your property out there. Them wolves, they're having a good time with him though. I don't think he's gonna be causing you any trouble for a bit. Heard tell his boy is dead." She had heard that too, and felt sorry for the man. "He took it hard, they said. You be careful. You don't need to be getting caught up in his mess either."

"I won't. I was wondering, Davie, if you need a job. Working for me? I'm going to open this place up with some home cooking. And to be honest with you, I'm not sure that people will go for it. Do you think you could come in once or twice a day and try things out for me? I'd pay you." He stared at her, then shook his head. "All right. But I promise you, it won't be too bad. I'm a fairly good cook."

"I ain't telling you no, darlin', but just shaking my head that you'd think that your cooking ain't fit to eat. That mate of yours, he's been praising you for days now, and I'd be a durn fool for not coming in and having me a meal or two of it." She grinned at him and he laughed. "If you don't beat all. Yes ma'am, I'll be in to have a meal or two. And if you see your way fit to have me in while you're working on the place, I'd do that too. Even if it's only to keep you company."

"I'd like that. Thank you, Davie." He nodded and moved on, talking about the meals he was going to have, and even telling himself what she'd said to him. She was watching him when she glanced at Elissa. She was smiling too. "He's a nice man, and is going to help me out."

"I heard. You should also know that he's not spoken so much as a single word to anyone directly in about ten years. Talks to himself a great deal, curses around people when they get in his way, but he's never, not in all the years I've known him, had a talk, much less an entire conversation. You did

152

well, my dear. Very well indeed." Quinn flushed and went back to her seat. "You might just be able to save his life, too. He's getting too old to be living out in the cold come winter. Perhaps you can persuade him to come inside enough to warm up."

"Yes, well, I'll see what I can do." Elissa asked if she was finished for the day or did she have more looking around to do. "No, I can be done. I was thinking that we should call the other women in and have a nice dinner. I don't get to do that very much. And especially with such good company."

"Then it's a date." They were waiting on them to meet them when Elissa hugged her to her. "You are a joy, my dear. I'm so glad that you and Hanson found each other. Especially after the family he had. My goodness, they were horrid."

They were loading in the car to meet at the restaurant when she remembered that her sister was at home alone and went and picked her up. Elissa said that she was coming in with Kendrick and that they were ready for some food and fun. Quinn was so glad that they included her in things. It was good for them both to be thought of so highly.

The restaurant was packed but they were seated right away, and platters of little sandwiches and drinks were brought to them quickly. As they settled around the table, Quinn thought of how much she loved these people. They were fun and honest, as well as the nicest people she'd met.

"I've been thinking about your restaurant, Quinn. And I was wondering if you were set on what sort of design that you were going to go for." Quinn told her that she'd not thought of a design yet, and asked Cassie what she had in mind. "Well, I think you should have some of the paintings from the locals in the place. Without price tags, of course, and change them out once in a while with more. That way it would be sort of like a revolving art gallery."

"I love that idea." She did too. "And I had someone suggest that I go to auctions and the like to get the plates and such, like silverware and glasses, to be charming. I think it'll be much less expensive too. Don't you think?"

"Yes, what a splendid idea. Oh, I love that." Elissa said she knew of a couple of indoor auctions that might be just the ticket. "We might not be able to get much right now, but it'll be a start. I love going to them, myself. Just so I can pick up a few books that I haven't read, as well as a painting or two. Yes, I think that'll be fun for us both."

After ordering, very proud of her sister for doing such a good job, they started talking about school and where Carmine was going to college should she want. It had never occurred to Quinn to think of such things at her young age, but apparently Carmine had. She was listing off the colleges that she wanted to attend, as well as some of the things they offered to their students. By the time their dinners arrived, it was obvious that her sister wanted to be a doctor.

When Davie came in and sat down, no one said a word. He was agitated a little, and she asked him if he was all right. He shook his head and started talking about men and what they were doing in his town.

"They've been lurking about. Like some of them snakes you see on television. You know the ones, Du, they're the ones that hurt people simply because they can." Quinn asked him if they'd hurt him. "Not me, no, but they're going to be standing out there when you leave here. You got yourself some protection in these women, but you need yourself a man here. Call them in."

She looked around the table and saw that the others seemed to be concerned now too. She asked Davie if it was the man who had lost his son. He told her that it was, and that he was coming for them. All of them.

Within minutes not only was Danburn there with the other men, but so was Danielle. She stood by her sister without moving. Sentry…that was the word that came to mind, she was a sentry watching her sister. Danielle looked at Danburn, and Quinn wondered if she was going to cause some trouble.

"I'd like to speak to you, sir." Danburn asked if it could wait. "Yes, my lord, it can, but I must tell you now that I am pledging myself to you and all that you are."

"All right. As soon as we're home again, I'd like to speak to you." She bowed and thanked him. "Thank you, Danielle, and welcome to the family."

She didn't see the man until Davie stood up. He looked very regal standing there. She had no idea why her thoughts went there. He was dressed in a dirty shirt and worn out shoes. His hair was dirty and could have used a good cutting, but regal was what she thought of.

"Here he comes." He moved into the restaurant like he owned the place. The man looked around, just staring at people before the hostess came to seat him. When he did, sitting about as far from them as he could have, Davie told them to go. "You run on out of here and I'll keep him busy. I'm good at that. Talking out of my head."

Telling him to be careful, she and Carmine moved out of the place. She was standing on the sidewalk when a large limo pulled up. She was helped inside with Carmine, and off they went.

~~~

His son was gone. Ramon sat down in the booth and tried to remember if he was leaving or just coming in. His heart just wasn't into having a meal, and he looked at the waitress when she asked him if he was ready to order.

"I was supposed to meet someone here." She asked him what their name was. "I'm not entirely sure. I've had a bad... Carmine. Her name is Carmine Langley. She has a sister named Quinn."

"They just left." He looked around the restaurant and then back at the waitress when she cleared her throat. "Lord Danburn, he called his car to come for them because he found out that someone was coming for the little girl."

That would have been him, he supposed. But how did they know he was coming? Regardless, he was going to get her. More determined than ever now, he asked who Lord Danburn was.

He was a big man. Ramon wasn't small, not by any means, but this man was as tall as anyone he'd ever come to know, and broad as well. Not fat...he was sure there wasn't an ounce of the stuff on him. And from the looks of him right now, he'd bet that fat would have been afraid to be on him. He was stern looking, like he was pissed off at the world. And he seemed to be staring right at him.

"Does he always look like that?" She asked him what he meant. "You know. Sort of like he could eat people for a living and not think a thing of it."

"Oh no. Lord Danburn promised the town that he'd not eat anyone here. Also, he will replace any sheep or cattle that he eats. He's been good to his word too." Ramon wondered if she was kidding, but then she started again. "A couple of years ago, I think it was, there was a problem with the cattle coming up missing. Mr. Hodges, he lost almost all of his. But Lord Danburn replaced them for him. And come to find out, it was someone else just taking them. Not his lordship for food."

"Seriously?" She smiled and told him that she was, then asked him what he wanted for dinner. "Just a salad, I guess. With some of that pie later. I've just lost my son."

"I'm sorry. If you'd like, you can ask Lord Danburn if he would help you find him." He told her that his son had died. "Oh, I'm so sorry. I misunderstood you. I'm terribly sorry. I'll get your order right in for you."

He wondered if she was a little touched in the head. To think that he lost his son and he'd not passed made him think that she was. Turning back to look at the stern man, he noticed that he was gone, but there was another man sitting at the table. Before he could turn back, the man started walking toward him and sat down at his table.

"You're Mr. Packer." Ramon said that he was. "I'm Hanson McClain. Quinn is my wife. I'd like to tell you, warn you, that you should stay away from her and her sister. I'd very much hate for you to end up on the wrong end of trouble."

There wasn't any point in denying it. He was there for the girl. Someone had told him that they'd seen her go into the place. But to have this man know, whoever he was, that he wanted the child wasn't anything that he wanted advertised.

"I don't know what you're going on about, but that kid is worth a great deal of money. I'm sure you know that." Hanson said nothing. "And I only want to talk to her. You can't blame a man for that, can you? I mean, her mom nearly.... She offered to sell her to me."

"Did she? Well, that's not what she told us before she died. She said that she called the office for advice, nothing more." Ramon agreed with that, but said there was more to it. "No, there wasn't. You've taken it upon yourself to go after her. And perhaps selling her off to the highest bidder. That won't do either."

"There are a lot of people that know I'm here." Hanson shook his head. "How are you so sure about that? For all you know, I have a recording device on me right now, and am recording every threat you make toward me."

He wished that he did have something to record the threats, but it was too late for that now. So Ramon lifted his chin up, trying for bravado rather than fear. Hanson stared at him for several seconds before laughing, so loudly that every patron in the room turned to stare at them.

"First of all, Ramon, that wasn't a threat, but I promise you that you come near my family, in any way shape or form, and I will kill you. Secondly, if I hear about you asking where any of them are, their whereabouts when they're in town, I'll come after you." He stood up, and it seemed to Ramon that he grew several inches as he did so. "You can also bet that when I do come for you, there will be nothing left of you. Not one hair to identify you, not a single drop of blood for DNA, and nothing left for dental records to try and figure out who the hell you were."

When Hanson walked away, Ramon sat there. He was pretty sure that every word of what the younger man had said was gospel. Not a single threat, but facts. As soon as his salad was set in front of him, he had a feeling that someone had spoken to the young woman too. She was decidedly hostile toward him.

"Here's your salad. And I've boxed up your pie too. I didn't know what you wanted, so you got apple." The pie was set down violently, and she glared at him. "If you don't mind leaving now, I've got to turn this table. After I disinfect it. People like you, bad people, shouldn't be allowed to frequent places where nice people eat. And your check has been taken care of. Goodbye."

He didn't bother eating the salad. Nor did he take the pie. Whatever had happened in here, he was sure that eating anything would have been his last meal. Getting up, he made his way to the front door and out before anyone else could speak to him. He was nearly to the funeral home again when he realized that not only did he not get the girl, but it seemed that the entire town knew about him. That could not be good.

The director was kind to him. He suggested that he have a closed casket, as well as only a few hours for calling. Most people would come by only to see how he'd died, being so young, and not pay any respects. He agreed with him. After the dinner thing, he was sure that it was all over the town that he wasn't anyone who should be associated with.

There would be no calling hours, he decided. Just a graveside service. Ramie had few friends, and the ones that he did have wouldn't come to it anyway. There would be flowers, he was told, and was asked how he wanted those taken care of, and Ramon wasn't sure.

"How about we donate them to the local nursing home? They'll love the treat, and no one will know who they came from. If that's all right with you?" Ramon agreed, anything that would get this over with. "The police department has let us take the body of your son, sir. And by tomorrow afternoon, we can have him ready. You just tell me a date, and then we'll work from there."

"As soon as possible." He nodded and said that was very good. "And if you'll bill me, I'd be able to pay it out with my insurance money. I had some taken out on him a few years ago."

"I'm sorry, sir, but that won't be necessary. His services have been paid for by Lord Danburn." He asked him why he'd do something like that. "I'm sure that I don't know, but he does that for people sometimes. It's a very good thing that he does. It so helps people out."

"Did he say why he'd do that for me? I mean, I got the impression that he didn't much care for me." The man told him that he didn't like him, but that didn't stop him from paying. "That's just nonsense. Why would he pay for someone's funeral services when he doesn't like them?"

"Perhaps he just wants you to leave town after this, and doesn't want you to not have the funds." Shocked would have been an understatement on how he felt at that moment. When the man stood up, so did Ramon. "Now, if there is nothing else, I'll show you out. I have a great deal of work to be done today if we're going to bury your son soon. You go home, sir, and pack. At least that's what I'd do. I'll see you soon."

He wasn't sure how it happened, but Ramon found himself out on the sidewalk with his coat in his hand and his hat askew on his head. Things were very strange. First he was warned off by a man of money. Then a waitress nearly tossed him out on his ass, and now this. A funeral director tells him that he needs to go home and get the hell out of town. As he walked home, he thought of the girl and the kid.

He'd lost his contact with the man he'd been working with. Not only did he tell him he was full of dung—his words, not Ramon's—but he also told him that he'd get himself in deep trouble if he went about lying about such things again. Ramon figured once he got the girl, there would be a line of people wanting a piece of her, but right now, he was going to need to take her before he could make anything.

"Ramie, you sure screwed things up for me." He looked around, wondering if anyone heard him when he saw a dirty old man. He was talking to himself, mumbling about food and dragons as he moved by him. Ramon wondered what that was about, but didn't let it bother him. He'd known a few nut balls in his time.

When he got home, he had seen the old man a total of four more times. Each time he spoke about what he was doing, watching, and that the dragon king was his friend. There wasn't anyone that he knew he should contact about him, and figured that he was more harmful to himself than others. Going inside, he watched out the window for twenty minutes, the man pacing down the street once more before he was gone. Ramon went to the living room and sat down. It had been a very stressful couple of days, and this man wasn't even a dip in the ocean as a concern for him.

Chapter 12

Hanson laid the phone back in the cradle and leaned back in his chair. In three weeks there would be a crew coming here to start on the work for his new plant. He was as excited about that as he had been when he opened his doors. There was a need for celebration, and just as he was going to find Quinn and see if she had time to join him, the three men from the Dragon Board appeared in his office. He sat down slowly and waited. Danburn came in the room just as he was ready to ask what was going on now.

"Your parents are deceased." He said that he knew that. "Their dragons have been sent to Mother Earth, and she has dealt with them as well."

"Yes, I'm aware of that. Is there a problem?" The first man said no, the second shrugged, and the third man just smiled. "That isn't very helpful."

"Nay, no trouble. You are well then?" Hanson looked over at Danburn when he laughed. "We are stalling, my lord. We're awaiting one more person to join us."

Quinn came in the room about fifteen minutes later. She

wasn't happy, he could see it on her face, and when number three asked her if she was all right, Hanson waited for her to blast the poor man.

"No, I'm not all right. I was in the middle of talking to my contractor, the man who charges two hundred dollars an hour outside of regular working hours to speak to me. I was so excited, and because of you making me come here, I've got to reschedule it and hope that I can get things started." Hanson nearly laughed at the expression on Three's face. "You had better have a good reason for making me come here."

"We do. I promise you." She crossed her arms over her chest and started tapping her foot. "There is a matter of the money that was in the safe. There is a great deal of it, even after the money used for their fines were taken out for their death."

"I'm to understand that Hanson paid his parents' fees and fines. What could you be taking from him now?" Danburn was the strongest dragon he knew. And when he spoke, people of all kinds listened. The Board took a step back when he stood up and continued. "If there is a problem, you can bet that I'll get to the bottom of it."

"No, no problem, but this is a fee, one that we take from each dragon when they are no longer alive." Quinn pointed out that they were no longer dragons when they died. "No, they were not. But they were at one time."

"You're not making the least bit of sense. Either they were or weren't dragons, and if not, then there was no reason for you to take a fee. That's robbing the dead." Three stretched his neck and looked at One and Two. If they had names, they didn't share them, and Hanson was happy with the names he'd given them. "How much are you stealing from the estate by calling it a dragon fee when they weren't dragons?"

164

"You see, we've been taking this money forever, miss." Quinn told him she was Hanson's mate and the holder of one of the dragons. "You have one? We were to understand that the earth had them."

"She gave them to me and to Kendrick, the mate to Danburn." One and Two simply disappeared, leaving Three all alone. He knew it too, as he looked around several times for someone to come and back him up or to rescue him. "Shall I show you mine?"

Hanson couldn't help it, he lost it when Three disappeared as well, leaving not only the decree that he had with him, but one of his shoes. And a fine shoe it was. It made Hanson wonder what the money was really going for in the name of fees. He showed it to Danburn, who was laughing hard enough to have tears running down his face.

"I'll have someone look into this. These men, they're only a part of the Board. But there are ones that are more in tune with what might be going on." Danburn looked at Quinn with a bow. "I have learned a great deal about you. You aren't as timid, nor as much of a pushover, as you were when you first came here. I like this version of you. So long as I'm not the one you're aiming your temper at."

"He is stealing money from a lot of people. Can you please look into that as well?" He told her that Noah would be pleased to do that for them. "He's a nice man to have around. I hope that you tell him how much you appreciate him."

"He is forever reminding me how much I need him. Trust me on that one." They all three laughed and Danburn stood up. "I have a meeting with Danielle this morning. If you don't mind, I'd like for you to be there. She's afraid of me, I think. Well, not of me, but of my station. Will you?"

"Yes, but if you bully her, I'm not going to sit still for it."

Danburn looked a little pissy, then smiled at her. "See? You wanted to yell at me too, didn't you?"

"You are much like my own mate. She won't let me get away with much either. And before I forget, the men have started on your building this morning. They are making good progress too." She thanked him and stood nearer to him. "If you have time now, we can get this meeting over with."

They were all going. Hanson had a few things to see to in town, as well as looking into a building or two in the town proper. He didn't really need it, but Cassie had told him that there were several that were up for sale, and instead of letting the city dictate who was able to use them, he should purchase them from the town. He thought it an excellent idea.

Opting out of the meeting, he met with Cassie and Noah at the first of the four buildings. Sadly, it needed to be torn down. It wasn't just structurally unsound, but was full of vermin, mice mostly, that might have spread to other buildings close by. Mice hated dragons and pretty much anything else that came around, but Cassie had a connection with such things and moved them along to the mountains. Hanson was reasonably sure that in a few days they'd be food for the other creatures there too.

The second building was in good shape, and he could see it being renovated easily. He was on the third floor of the structure when Noah approached him. The man was a wonder, yet he seemed to be in a mood today. Waiting on him to speak first, Hanson moved around the office-like rooms until he was ready.

"I should like to speak to you about your household, my lord." Hanson leaned against the windowsill and asked him what he meant, as he had no staff. "Precisely. You are in need of staff. A cook for when the young miss is working at her business. A housekeeper for the household when the children come, as well as a workforce for the yard."

"And who have you hired for these positions?" Noah looked like he was going to lose his temper, but calmed a little before he did. Laughing, Hanson spoke. "You have a way about you, don't you, Noah? And since I know you so well, why don't you just send them to the house and we can meet them? Or have you already sent them on their way?"

"They're a good reliable group, my lord." Hanson said he knew that. "It is unfitting for someone in your station to be left to pick up after yourself. Also, there are a great many people out of work now. The factory that employed the masses is closing down, and they are laying off a large portion of their employees every week. And it's so close to Christmas."

"Why are they closing up?" He only shrugged. "Come on, Noah, you know the reason. Like you know that I should buy the three buildings here even though they're not really in that good of shape."

"We are in need of a hospital. Not just a clinic, but an actual hospital. There is also a need for a department store. Not the sort that sells dishes that cost more for one place setting than most of the people make in one day, but a cheaper version of it. Also, and I think you would agree with me, we're in dire need of a place for entertainment. For the younger people. And I would like to see an ice cream shop." Hanson cocked his brow at the last one. "I have found that I enjoy the cold treat. And it has been my greatest pleasure sharing it with the young miss. Lady Carmine, she is very childlike for one so old, don't you think?"

"You mean because she's so strong in her abilities, you think that makes her old." Noah told him he thought her to have an old soul. "Yes, I can see that. But as you pointed out, she is very much a child. All right, Noah, you'll have your list. But you have to help me out with it. I know of no one to run such operations."

"I have a list of those names as well." Hanson laughed. "The pack, my lord, it is filled with young people biting at the bit to have a job in the bigger cities. This will be just the ticket in getting them to stay here for their families. Also, if you don't mind me saying this, when your own children come along, you'll want someone that has some experience with shifters and such."

The next buildings were in better shape. He looked at and purchased a total of six in the area; the other three were for sale by a realtor. Hanson thought he'd made a few people happy, but less so with the downtown committee. They had plans for the buildings as well. And he didn't think it was to help the people.

As he finished up paying for the buildings and putting his claim in for them at the courthouse, he was approached by Mrs. Cunnings, a woman that he'd never cared for...and cared less for her sons. She poked him in the chest with her cane when she stood in front of him.

"I had it in mind to buy that building on Tenth, Mr. McClain. You have cock blocked my plans." He told Mrs. Cummings that he had plans as well. "I'm sure you think you do. Now, let's deal, why don't we? I'll give you ten percent over the amount you paid for it. Right now."

"No. It's not for sale." She told him that everything and everyone had a price. "No, I don't. Now, if you'll excuse me, I have to gather a crew together to get started."

"Twenty percent. Come now, a man like you, you could use a little extra cash with that new wife and child. Twenty-five and not a penny more."

He turned and walked away. She was shouting more numbers at him as he made his way out the door. "Noah?" He said that he would look into it. "Thank you. I don't know what her deal is, but there is something going on. And let me know whatever it is you find out."

"I will, my lord. She was most insistent, don't you think?" He pointed out that it could be nothing, but Noah shook his head. "I will find out. And when I do, we'll think about how to fix it. And if you don't mind, we should put extra care into the building as well."

"Yes, you might be right on that." He made his way out of the courthouse and they went to the restaurant on Tenth. "Look over there, Noah. She's in the building now."

They watched her carefully and noted that she had brought a crew to work on it as well. Noah asked what they were going to do. Hanson told him for now, he was going to keep an eye on her. In less than ten minutes a large semi pulled up and started unloading material to work on the building. That was when he stood up to approach the woman.

"What are you doing?" The police were being called by Noah, and Hanson thought he was having a good time with this situation. "You and I just spoke, and you know that I own this place."

"Yes, but we'll come to an understanding, you and I. I don't want to waste a moment on getting repairs done." Marty got out of his car along with two of his men. "You called the police? Whatever for? My goodness, you're making a mountain out of nothing more than a mole hill. We can't discuss business if you're going to be nasty about it."

"I'm not the one moving in on a building that someone else owns." Marty shook his hand and he told him what was going on. "She knows that I own it…she was at the courthouse when I paid the fees for it."

"Mrs. Cunnings, I think you need to move on." She told him that they were working here today. "No, you're not. You're not the owner, and this man isn't going to sell to you. Call them off or I'll have to arrest you."

"But they're coming soon." He asked her who was coming about the time that Danielle showed up. After bumping against Mrs. Cunnings, she smiled at him. "You need to sell me this building, young man. I'm no longer kidding around with you."

"There is a group coming in to buy up downtown. They wish to revitalize it into something bigger and better. Or so they say." Hanson asked Danielle who they were. "A group of men who come into small towns, buy up buildings that are falling into disrepair, and sell them to the community with the promise of making them livable as well as modern. Then they leave them holding the bag on taxes and such without finishing any of the started repairs. She is well aware of this, as her son is a part of the group."

"You lie." Mrs. Cunnings turned to him. "She has no idea what she's talking about. I don't have to stand here and listen to this. You've insulted me to the point where I don't wish to deal with you. You'll sell me this building right now and I'll forget the entire thing."

"I'm not selling. I've told you this several times now. And if you continue on this trend, then I'll have you arrested for trespassing." She huffed at him and Hanson laughed. "You'll leave now or so help me, I'll forget that I'm a gentleman."

"You are no such thing. Wait until my son hears about this. Don't think he's going to be as nice as I am about how you've treated me."

She went away, but the crew stood there waiting. He

170

didn't know what they were supposed to do now, so he hired them on the spot, so long as they did what he wanted and not Mrs. Cunnings. Most of them, he knew, were part of Shawn's pack. As they made their way back to the restaurant, Noah was laughing. He was glad that he'd made someone's day with this.

~~~

As soon as Danielle returned to the house, she told them what had happened. Danburn didn't seem upset by the actions of the other woman, but he did say that he'd had trouble with her before. Danielle sat back down in her chair and waited. Quinn wasn't sure what happened next, as Danburn had already taken her pledge.

"Carmine will be your only charge in this." Danielle said that she could help others as well. "Yes, I'm aware of that, and I thank you for it. But Carmine will be your first priority. All right?"

"Yes. She is a good girl. Sometimes too strong for her own good. But I will protect her with my life." Danburn asked her why. "Because I have pledged to do so."

"That's not what I mean and you know it. You and her, you have a connection somehow. What happened that brought you here, and why her? I'm not saying that I don't appreciate you doing this for us, but tell me why you have such a closeness to her." Quinn saw the vampire's face heat up and wondered about it. "I can't allow anything to happen to any of my family, Danielle, so if there is something that I should know, you need to tell me."

"She saved my life, my lord. When I was being tied to the ground, she came to my aid. Despite the others there that wished for me to be dead." Quinn asked her when this was. "Several months ago now, or perhaps a year, I was caught

171

out feeding and they wished to have sport with me. Sex too. But I was too…I didn't allow that. But they did tie me down. Carmine came out of the darkness and cut me loose, with the promise that I'd not seek revenge on them. She said that they'd be taken care of."

"She did something to them." Danielle said that they'd done it themselves. "I don't understand. My sister can do a great many things to people without them knowing about it."

"She did nothing to these men. Two nights after I was released, they were out on a boat. The boat capsized and they drowned. All of them." Quinn nodded, still not sure that it hadn't been Carmine. "She promised me, my lady, that she did nothing to them. That the weather had turned and as they were in their cups, they did not heed the warnings."

Still, she could have done that, and Quinn was worried about her. Danielle said that she was in need of going to bed and they let her. When Danburn asked her if she needed anything from him, she thought he was running her off, and told him she'd get out of his hair. He laughed.

"Nay, I wish to have a conversation with you for a bit. It's about Christmas. My mom, she said that she spoke to you about breakfast." Quinn smiled and said that she had. "You don't have to if you don't want. My mom can be quite persuasive when she wants something. I love her more than words could ever say, but she is pushy too."

"No, I want to. It'll give me some practice in cooking for larger groups, and I can try out some things on you guys too. Also, I told her that I'd be making some dinners. If you think you guys would like to come?" He laughed and said she'd have trouble keeping them away. "That'll be wonderful. I have some ideas that I think you might enjoy. But I need a promise that you'll be honest with me about the meals. I can't have people coming to me later and saying that something is wrong with them. I'm hoping that cooking like I like will be enough to keep the restaurant going."

"Have you thought of a name yet?" She said that the others had been peppering her with ideas for a few days now. "Yes, I had a guess that they might. Kendrick likes Dragon's Lair, but you pick what you wish. It'll be a good name that I think will reflect on your tastes. Also, I heard that you hired Du."

"Yes, but he goes by Davie when he's with me. He's a nice old man." Danburn agreed with her. "And for some reason, he means something to me. A connection that I can't understand."

"Perhaps because he's been around nearly as long as me." She asked how that was possible. "He was, at one time, a dragon watcher. Few know that. I don't even think that my mom is aware of what he was. His master is gone now, died a great many years ago and left him alone. There are not very many of his kind around. You're very lucky to have him."

"He doesn't belong to me." Danburn said in Davie's mind, he more than likely did. "I don't know what to do about him now."

"Nothing. He will serve you, much like he has now. And he will protect you, in the same way that my staff protects me. Not by sword, though at one time I believe that he could have swung one. And he's an immortal that will be able to help you with questions that you might not have formed in your mind as yet." She asked him what that meant. "When you're indecisive about something, such as the name of your place, he'll know that and let you bounce them off him. Then when you've decided, he'll put words to action. He'll serve you well, as I have said."

Quinn wasn't sure what to think of that, but when she left Danburn to his business, she went to the work area at her restaurant. They were working very hard, and she didn't want to get in their way so decided to go up to the upper levels of the building and look around. There wasn't a lot of stuff up there, but she did enjoy going through some of it.

"There you are." She looked at Carmine and asked her what she was up to. "I was on my way to the house when I had a feeling that you'd be here. Whatcha doing?"

"Nothing really. Just having a look around. I have to go through this stuff so they can toss out what I don't want while the dumpsters are here." Carmine asked if she could help. "Of course you can. And anything you want, go ahead and take it. I saw some books over there in the corner yesterday."

They'd worked together for about an hour when Carmine called her over. She had found the books apparently, and had them spread out all over the floor. When she held one of them up for her to look at, Quinn was surprised by the title of it.

"*How to Dissect a Dragon*. That's sort of eerie, don't you think?" Carmine laughed and it made her smile. "What do you suppose that thing was doing up here? I mean, there has always been a good bond between Danburn and the townspeople."

"It's not what you think. It's a book about their way of thinking and how their mind works so differently than a human's does. It's not very good. I've been reading some of it, and it says that the dragon is mean all the time and has a lust for bloodletting." She sat down next to her sister as she continued. "It also says that while they're very wealthy, they didn't earn their money the correct way, and that most of them are only rich by their tears. Do you have tears that turn to gems?"

174

"Yes. I mean, I guess so. I've not had a reason to cry yet while a dragon." Carmine told her that according to the books, she could cry as a human and have them as well…they were smaller, however. "I'll have to keep that in mind when I'm upset. What else did you find?"

"Some old dishes that you might want to use downstairs. And some bowls to serve in. I've been meaning to ask you, are you going to do this plate style or family? There are a lot of people that I think could benefit from the family way of doing it. You could maybe give them a choice." She liked that idea and asked her if she thought she should have a family night. "Yeah, that way you'd have only big families coming in rather than just a single person here or there."

They looked over the dishware and put it aside. When Quinn heard Carmine's belly growl, Quinn asked her if she wanted to go home or eat here in town. They opted for town and made their way toward the restaurant.

The explosion of pain in the back of her head knocked her to the sidewalk. Dizzy, she tried to stand and put her hand to her head. Blood was all over her and she looked for her sister. It didn't take her long to realize that she'd been taken. Reaching for Hanson, she closed her eyes again. It wasn't until someone was standing over her that she realized she'd passed out.

"My sister. I think that asshole took her." Hanson helped her stand up. He told her to be careful, she was bleeding pretty badly. "I have to find her. He's taken her."

"Danielle is awake and looking for her now. She'll be able to find her, but not help. It's too hot in the day for her to go after her right now. But she isn't harmed, nor has she been drugged. They're talking." Quinn wasn't sure how that was helpful, but said nothing. "She said to tell you that she's sorry that she's failed you so badly."

"She hasn't failed me at all. I want Carmine home, but not at the risk of making Danielle hurt when we can go and get her. We can, right?" Hanson said that they would. "I don't want either of them hurt. Not like this. What did he hit me with?"

"It looks like he used a ball bat. And to be honest with you, honey, had you been human, he would have killed you. I'm pretty sure that was his plan." Quinn was feeling better and told him that. "That's the dragon in you. Healing you faster than normal. As soon as you feel like it, we'll get going. We don't have a location as yet, but Danburn is looking, as well as Cassie. We'll find her soon."

"I hope so. She and I have plans for the Lair. She can't be hurt or gone from me." Hanson said that he understood. "Also, I don't know how this works, but I want to have a baby sometime. Soon if we can."

"I'd love that as well." Hanson laughed. "You sure have timing, I'll give you that. We'll get your sister back, taken care of the bad guy, and make a baby. Not necessarily in that order, but that's the plan."

She was pretty sure he was making fun of her, but she was just too upset to care. As soon as they heard from Danielle, the rest of the family came to them. It was going to be war, she thought. No one touched what was hers and got away with it.

Chapter 13

Ramon was giddy. It had gone much better than he had hoped. Not only did he have the girl, but he'd killed off the woman too. There would be no one coming after him for this. The man who had threatened him wouldn't do much at all in his grief. Dancing a little jig around the basement, he looked at the girl when she laughed too.

"And what do you find so funny? In case you didn't notice, I've got you just where I want you. And I'm selling you off to the highest bidder." She just sat there and continued to smile. "You won't think it's so funny when I have your mind hooked up to some machine where they suck your brain dry."

"You're dumber than I thought if you believe that. And you'll not have a chance to sell me off to anyone. My family will be here soon, and they'll take care of you." He laughed, sure that she was full of shit. "My sister isn't dead either. She's the one organizing the search for me."

"I don't think so, kid. I hit her as hard as I could. And there was enough blood spilling out under her that she won't have survived that." He laughed again. "You owe me, you know. And I aim to collect."

"My mom was only asking questions when she called there. You should have just left well enough alone." He ignored her, but it didn't shut her up. "What did she say to you, anyway that made you think that I was worth anything?"

"She said that she had this kid that could move things with her head. Her mind, she told me, was strong, and she wondered what would cause that." The kid nodded as if she already knew that. "So, being me, the smart man that I am, I started asking her questions. Like how big a thing could you move and such. She said that you moved a car once."

"Yes, it was in our way when we were parked. It was the first time that I showed her what I could do." He hadn't known that but didn't really care. "Did she tell you that I could move things like knives and saws? Like the ones you have hanging down here?"

He looked around the room with that in mind. There were a lot of things in here that he'd never thought of as weapons to be used against him. His only thought was that he wanted to hide her away someplace where nobody could see her. When she laughed again, he asked her what was so funny.

"You are. Suddenly so afraid, aren't you? Well, you don't have any reason to be afraid of me. Not yet at any rate. But when the dragons get here, you're going to be toast. Quite literally." He asked her what she was talking about. "The man that you met the other day, my stepdad? He's a dragon. So is Lord Danburn and the other men with him. They're coming too. All of them are."

"You're nuts. There isn't any such thing as a dragon." She didn't say anything more, and he wondered if he should ask her about them. "You don't know anything. You're just trying to scare me into letting you go. But I'm not going to. I have

178

plans for you, and it's going to make me some money."

"You'll be making nothing from me but an early grave." He shivered. Her voice had suddenly turned cold, hard even. Like she was a grown up, not a little girl. "And would you like to know what else? No one will care at all that you're no longer around."

He believed her. Not only that, he was also tempted to let her go with the promise that she didn't come after him. But he was pretty sure that's what she wanted from him. To be freed and to be left alone. But he was smarter than her. She was a kid that didn't know the workings of an adult.

The sounds on the upper levels made him nervous. Going up the stairs after making sure that the kid was secured, he was careful that he was quiet. As soon as he looked in the peephole in his door, he laughed a little. The mail lady standing there had given him the willies. Opening the door, he smiled at her.

"I need your signature on a couple of things. You have some registered mail." He told her that was fine and took her pen. "How you been holding up, Mr. Packer? I heard about your son killing himself."

"He was a troubled mind." She nodded, but didn't say she was sorry or anything, like most would have done. "He was all I had in the world."

"I knew him. He wasn't a very smart boy, was he?" He thought her rude for saying that and told her. "I'm sure that there are a lot of people thinking the same thing as me. I noticed that there wasn't a group of people at his funeral yesterday. Maybe that should tell you something."

"I should report you for being so rude to me." She shrugged. "You don't care that you might lose your job over this? Are you so rich that you don't need it? I'd think you'd

179

have better manners than to say something like that to a man who just lost his son."

"You'd think that, but I don't care. And if you ask anyone here, they'd say the same thing. We all know what you're about. And while you've been here telling me bull, the others have gone in the back way and are waiting for you." She took the pen and paper and stuffed it in his mailbox. "You have a good day, Mr. Packer. It's been nice knowing you."

He was almost afraid to turn around. He could hear them then, the people that had come in the back door. Turning slowly, still thinking of the dragons that the kid had told him about, he wasn't surprised to see the woman he'd hit sitting on his couch, and five men and a woman standing behind her. Ramon wanted to tell them they were trespassing, but he was ordered to sit.

"This is Danburn English. You've met him. And Hanson McClain, my mate. The others, Rett Welsh, Dana Blankenship, and Kip Newton, are friends of ours. Griffith Farley is in the basement freeing my sister. And this is Cassie Welsh. She isn't too happy with you either." Ramon asked them what they wanted. "My sister. And you dead. So you know, you will be soon enough. But I have a few questions you're going to answer."

"I don't have to answer anything." When someone snapped their fingers, he found himself flat on the floor with a weight on his back that was so painful, he cried out from it. "What are you doing to me? Let me go right this minute."

"There is no one touching you. We're all right here where you saw us before." He lifted his head and he could see them all. Not one of them had moved. "As you can see, we're not touching you. Perhaps there is something wrong with you?"

"There is nothing wrong with me. I'm fine. What I am

upset about is that you're in my house and you have no rights to be." The woman, he didn't remember her name, asked about her sister. "She's visiting me. I asked and she said she'd like to come and have a talk and some tea."

"Carmine doesn't like tea. Hot or cold, so that's your first lie. The second is that you asked her anything about coming here. You hit me and took her. The rag that you left behind when you drugged her is at the police station now. They're very unhappy with you too." He looked at the woman Cassie, then back at the one doing all the talking. "Also, you should know that I'm not going to kill you. I'm not allowed. Carmine thought it would haunt me for the rest of my days. She's probably right…she usually is."

He was relieved, so much so that he sat up and then moved to a chair. It was nice not feeling like he'd been stapled to the floor and able to face them on his level. Once he was there, he noticed that the kid had joined them. He wasn't happy about that, but figured it was all right for now. Ramon had gotten her once, he'd have no problem getting her again. And this time he'd be more careful to kill any witnesses.

"Not to say that you won't be killed. It just won't be by me." He stared at her for several seconds, wondering what sort of person would say such a thing, even in jest. "You don't believe me, do you?"

"Nope. You're not the type of person that goes around killing people." She asked him if he was. "If given the right motivation, such as a great deal of money, I would imagine that anyone would under those circumstances."

"Like your son?" Ramon explained that it wasn't money that had motivated him, but love, or the lack of it. "You're saying that love drove him to kill himself. But for you, it would only be money? That's sort of sad, don't you think? To me,

181

love and the greed for money aren't even in the same realm as having a loved one threatened. To me, my sister means everything. Even money can't take that away from us."

"I bet that if I offered you ten million, you'd think about it." Quinn shook her head. "Not even a hundred million? You're lying. Everyone and everything has a price."

She stood up and he felt his balls curl up around his ass. When she stood over him, her breath almost too hot to be touching his face, she smiled at him. And it was then, at that very moment, that he knew that not only did she have it in her to kill him, but that she had a plan to do it.

"Not everyone, you'll figure out, has a price. Or if I have a price for my sister's life, which I do, then you'll get that better than anyone else. Your death is the only thing that I want for her. So not only will she be safe and free of men like you, but she can be a child again, with the freedom to make choices that she might not have been able to before you and your *help* to my mom." He wanted to make promises to her. Tell her that he'd leave them alone, but she moved back from him, and that was when he saw the others. "This is my family, Mr. Packer, and they're going to ensure that my sister and I are safe from men such as yourself."

She left him there, with the men and the woman. He wanted to laugh, to tell them this had been a fine joke, but that was all it was, a joke. But the look on the face of Cassie gave him pause. And when she lifted her hands and a dozen or so little bugs swarmed around her, he was confused.

"This is my army, Ramon Packer. And they're going to do what we cannot."

The first sting was like being stung by a large bee. He looked at the little bug and realized that it was a person...a wee, tiny little person. When she grinned at him, her teeth looking shark-like even as small as they were, he wanted to knock her away and leave there. But she moved in front of him, and he felt his body being turned inside out with pain.

They burrowed into him, surrounded him in dizzying speeds that made him ill. As they beat into his flesh, he looked down at his body and saw that they'd done just as he'd felt. They'd entered his body and left him with holes in his skin.

Blood pooled under his feet. His hands were soaked with it, so much so that he wasn't able to tell his hand from the blood beneath it. His head felt heavy, and his legs had no muscle to move. He couldn't have gotten up to run even if he'd had a mind to. As they entered his mind, buzzing right into his ears and neck, thoughts of dying this way were starting to scare him. Ramon looked up at the man in front of him and wanted to beg him to end him.

"You'll be dead soon enough. But before you are, I should like to show you what we are." The man disappeared, and in his place was a dragon. One so large that he fell through his floor to the lower level, his head so large that the ceiling and roof above them crumbled in a pile of rubble of wood splinters and slate from the roof. Falling into the sub levels with the man, he knew that he was nearing death. Everything hurt beyond what he thought a person could or should be able to stand.

"Kill me. Please?"

The dragon spit a bit of flames at him. They didn't do much more than ignite some of the wood, then sputter out.

Ramon could no longer speak. Something had happened to his tongue and his eye. Looking at the dragon that stood well above him, he tried to convey what he wanted and felt the flame of him, his hot breath, spray over him. Even as his flesh burned from his bones, Ramon knew that this wasn't the end of it. He was going to suffer.

~~~

Quinn sat on the back deck and looked out over the pool and trees. She had no idea how long she'd been there, hours she supposed, but still, she was in no hurry to go inside yet. And didn't want to see anyone that would require her to speak to them. Her mind, she thought, had had enough. When Hanson sat in the chair next to her, she didn't even acknowledge him. But for some reason, he seemed to understand that she didn't want to speak.

"When I was a young dragon, there was a group of humans that came upon our play area. My sister and I would go out there daily, shifting into dragons and playing with the stones there. When a dragon heats a stone, it will stay warm for a decade. You might someday need to remember that. Anyway, we were playing around and these men came upon us." He reached for her hand and she took it, feeling the lifeline of it like an anchor in her mind. "Jessie was always braver than I was, and she shifted back to being a human and sat near one of the stones we'd been playing with. The men, all of them younger than us by many years, started to touch her. Poking her with their fingers and hands until she turned on them. I thought for sure she was going to burn them alive, but she only stared at them."

"You didn't help her? What kind of brother leaves their sister to fend off a group of stupid men?" He told her to hush, it was his story. "Yes, well, it's a shitty one if you ask me."

"I didn't, now be quiet. Anyway, she turned and stared at these men for several minutes until they backed from her. Jessie took two steps toward them when they took one back. She was very brave to do such a thing, and I was proud of her. But the men, they were mean and had only one thing in mind

184

about a young woman out alone." She turned and looked at him, waiting for him to tell her what Jessie had done. "Did you get enough dinner? I loved the lobster rolls you made. My goodness, you are so good in the kitchen."

"Stop it." He asked her what he was doing. "Tell me what she did. I need to know that they didn't hurt her."

"They didn't. Not one of them came back to that area either, so you know." She stared at him, hard, knowing that she was going to have to get up and murder him soon if he didn't spill it. "I was behind her. As my dragon. None of them would have ever harmed her. And had they tried, there would have been nothing left of them. She, however, never knew that I'd helped her. But she was forever braver after that."

"You did help her." He nodded. "Was there a point to this story, or are you shining me on, as my sister does when she wants something?"

"She needs a new computer, by the way. But yes, there was a point. You went into that house terrified of a great many things. Not just that your sister was going to be hurt, but that you'd not be able to stand up to Packer. But not only were you able to, you also saved everyone there." She asked him how she'd done that. "Because had you not done what you did, said those things to the man in front of you, you would have been haunted, just as Carmine said, by his death. But since you were brave and stood up to him, you know that you did the best that you could and left us to end it for you. And your sister."

"But he's still dead." Hanson said that he was. "I know that it had to be done. That someone had to end his life so that we'd be safe, especially my sister, but that doesn't negate that he is dead, and by our hand."

"May I ask you a question?" She nodded at him. "Would

185

you have felt better about him being dead if you knew for sure that no one else is coming for the two of you? Because while I'd like to say that was true, I have no way of knowing one hundred percent that someone someday might not come around. However, I can promise you that so long as I'm able, which will be for a great many years, no one will ever harm the two of you without consequences."

She got up and went to him, sitting on the chair with him and curling her arms around his warm body. It was where she needed to be, where she had to be to deal with all this. And when she felt like she could speak about it without sobbing, she told him what else was bothering her.

"I told you that I was going home, that I didn't want to be there when he was killed. But I didn't. I heard him screaming and begging for someone to kill him. I heard the way he died, and I think it will haunt me for the rest of my life." He lifted her chin up and asked her to look at him. What she saw there made her want to hold him to her heart for the rest of her days. "I love you, Hanson McClain. More than I ever thought I could love a person. And you've made me so very happy. So happy that I don't want this to ever end."

"I love you as well, my love. More than I can ever put to words to you. But you'll forget this, and what was done and said today. You might not forget it completely, but there will be times when it comes to you and all you need to do is know that you made your family safe. All right?" Quinn nodded. "Good girl. Now, you mentioned something about a baby. I would love to work on that with you. But first, I have to shift and give you a scale. I'm told that it's the most assured way of you conceiving a dragon child."

"Will I have eggs?" He said that she would, but not Kendrick on this pregnancy. "Because she conceived before she was dragon."

"Yes. Cassie will have a dragon like herself. Because she is the dragon in the family, that's the only way she would birth a child." She said she was nervous. "About having a dragon? There is nothing to it. The only thing you must worry about is them burning down the house in the first few years of their lives. And teething will be a bitch, because they'll want to eat humans for that. Also, and few know this, when a baby dragon has a dirty diaper, when it's being changed, it will be like lava. At least for the first five years of their life."

She stared at him for several moments. Then she laughed. Christ, she loved this man, and the way he made her forget her sorrow for a time. Laying her head on his chest, she told him again how much she loved him.

"And I love you. But there are some things we'll have to talk about before we have a child. Things like keeping you hidden away for a time. And how the child will be born. There are people out there that would take advantage of your weakened condition when you birth a dragon." She asked if he'd be there. "Yes, all of us will. And Danburn will have a gift for him or her. Something magical."

"I just want it to be healthy and happy. And know that we'll love it for all time." She thought about his sister's dragon, and wondered what he was going to do with her. "I almost forgot, we're having Christmas breakfast here, and then we're all going to the castle for presents and dinner. I hope everyone will be okay with that."

"They are. And I invited Davie to join us. He said that he'd be here with his bells on. I'm pretty sure that he really will have bells on too. He showed them to me." Laughing, she closed her eyes and listened to the beating of his heart and the purr of his dragon. "Quinn, there are dragons all over the world, did you know that?"

"I figured there were more than just you guys. Why did you tell me that?" He nodded to the yard and she turned on his lap to see her. "Where did she come from, do you know?"

"No, I didn't see her until a few minutes ago. She's a green dragon." If she knew what that meant, she couldn't think about it right now. Turning slowly so as not to startle her, Quinn asked him if she was a shifter like them. "Yes. She's here to talk to Danburn. I called him here when I saw her."

Quinn stood up and approached the dragon. She wasn't much bigger than she was, but she was vicious looking. Her armor, what she knew covered their head and chest, was heavier and spiked. Even the spines along her back were sharper than even Danburn's were. As she got closer to her, she could also see that she'd been hurt. A long time ago, she guessed, as she was scared now. The shift from dragon to woman was quick and beautiful.

"My name is Emerald. I go by Em." Quinn told her who she was. "I have been hiding for a great long time, and have found that I cannot continue to do so. A friend of mine, Danielle, said that there was a safe haven for dragons here. That if accepted by Danburn, the king, I could live here without problems."

"To be honest with you, I'm not sure how that works." She looked to her right and Quinn turned too. "This is my mate, Hanson McClain. You're welcome here for as long as you need to rest. But Danburn is on his way."

"Thank you, my lady." Quinn asked her what kind of dragon she was. "Water dragon, my lady. I swim the seas and walk on land too. But I love the water."

"That's good. I know that there are places to swim around here, but again, you'll have to speak to Danburn." She nodded and simply fell to the ground.

Before she could get to her to help, she was knocked aside by something large, like an oversized dog. Then she realized it was a gryphon, like the ones in tales of creatures that weren't real. He stood in front of Em and growled low and ruffled up his feathers.

"He's my friend, and protector. He can be a bit overzealous at times, but he means well." Em put out her hand to the large animal and he moved toward her. "Come here, you overgrown cat, and tell the lady you are sorry. She was only trying to help me."

He purred then, the sound of it loud in the empty grounds around them. Quinn wanted to touch him, to run her fingers over his body to assure herself that he was real. When she was close enough to touch him, she felt rather than saw that Hanson had joined her.

The gryphon's head and front talons were that of an eagle. His wings, too, were those of the large bird and now tucked tightly against his body. The body of the great creature was that of a lion. His tail, now curled around his back paws, was thick and long. When he bowed his head before her, she touched her hand to his head and heard the purr grow louder.

"What's his name?" Em told her that he liked to be called Sebastian. "What a lovely name you have, sir. I am Quinn McClain. You are welcome to my home while your friend rests."

"Thank you, my lady." She'd not expected him to speak, and his voice was as deep and dark as his body. Quinn bowed to him, and he licked her hand and said that they were now connected as well. "You are also ready for breeding, should you wish a child. I can tell such things because I am a creature of the world. You and your mate, you'll have strong healthy dragons, whenever you wish to have them."

"We were just talking about that." Flushing hotly, she told him she was sorry. "I'm not usually so blunt. But you are welcome here for as long as you wish."

By the time Danburn and Kendrick showed up, they'd put Em to bed and had her looked over. Sebastian never left her side, and even when Danburn showed up, he was very protective of the dragon. She asked if they could stay.

"Yes. I should have mentioned she was coming a few days ago. I spoke to Danielle about her coming here, and told her that she'd be welcome." Quinn thanked him. "No need for that. I was hoping that more dragons would come around. This will be a safe place for any of them, should they make it here."

They were becoming quite the large family, she thought.

Chapter 14

Hanson waited for Rett to come to his offices. There were a few things that he needed to talk to him about, and a couple of jobs he wanted him to do for him. He liked the younger man, and was sure that he'd be good at them. Also, he was going to give him his sister's dragon.

If someone had asked him even a year ago if that was possible, he would have told them no. To him, when a shifter died then their counterpart died with them. And after talking to a couple of others and reading some of the history that Danburn had in his library, he'd found out a great deal more.

It didn't always work that way. The dragon would have to be not harmed when the person died. Like for instance, his sister's death. She'd been poisoned by iron. The human part of her had given up and died long before the poison had killed her dragon, thus leaving her alive when Jessie had passed. If her dragon had died, say in battle, then the human part of her would have succumbed to death as well. It was complicated.

Rett showed up blustering about the cold and the snow. It was a week before Christmas now, and Hanson knew that it was only going to get colder with more snow before spring came again. As soon as he was standing next to the fireplace and seemingly warming up, Hanson spoke.

"I'm giving you my sister's dragon." He might have worked up to it, he supposed, but to see the look on Rett's face was worth it. "She needs a human body, and I think you could use her well."

"I'm not a shifter." He said that he knew that, but neither had Kendrick or Quinn been one. "I guess I know that. But why me?"

"Because I trust you. I like you a great deal too. And you're part of this family." Rett thanked him. "Also, I think that having you as a dragon too, it will mean that you'll be around a lot longer. I know that you're an immortal, but you can still be hurt and killed. As a dragon, you'd have more strength, as well being able to heal from a great many more things than you can now."

"Thank you, I think. I mean, I do appreciate you thinking of me, but I can't help but think there are more deserving people out there." Hanson told him not as far as he was concerned. "I don't know what to say."

"You say, 'Thank you, Hanson, I'll take her.' But I might mention that she will become a male once she's in your body." He nodded, saying that he knew that from the others. "I want you to have her, Rett. For selfish reasons, I guess. I'll know that my sister's dragon is with someone that is kind and generous, as well as a good person."

"Thank you, Hanson, I'll take him...her from you." Nodding, Hanson asked him to have a seat. "What about the dragon? Do we have to do something?"

"It's done." Rett smiled, like he was the butt of a great joke. "No, really, he's there with you now. I can smell him."

"Seriously?" Hanson told him he was. "I have to go home. I mean, thank you, but I need to go home so that I can shift with.... Does Cassie know? I guess she wouldn't, would she?"

"I've not told her, but I'm sure she knows it now." He asked how. "She would know that you've been changed. I think that even Danburn knows by now. By the way, you'll have to go and pledge your dragon to him at some point."

Before he knew it, Hanson was sitting in his office all alone and laughing. Not only had Rett simply gotten up and left him in mid-sentence about what he wanted done, but he had left his briefcase and his coat. He was still laughing about it when Quinn came to see what was so funny.

"Well, I guess he's happy about it, don't you think?" He told her that he seemed very happy, in the few minutes he'd been there after the change. "I'm so glad that you did this. Not just for him, but for you as well."

Hanson warned the others about the new dragon in the form of Rett. Then he told them what had happened. Danburn said that he'd go looking for him if he didn't see him in a few days, and thanked him as well. It was going to be fun having someone else to fly with, and Hanson was looking forward to it.

Now he only had to take care of his new guest and her friend. After that, who knew what sort of trouble they'd have? And for once, Hanson was looking forward to things being… well, not normal, but different. Kissing his mate, he took her up to the bedroom to work on that new baby. The scale had done its part, he hoped, and now the rest was up to him and Quinn.

Before You Go...

HELP AN AUTHOR

write a review

THANK YOU!

Share your voice and help guide other readers to these wonderful books. Even if it's only a line or two your reviews help readers discover the author's books so they can continue creating stories that you'll love. Login to your favorite retailer and leave a review. Thank you.

AWARD WINNING, BESTSELLING AUTHOR

Kathi Barton, winner of the Pinnacle Book Achievement award as well as a best-selling author on Amazon and All Romance books, lives in Nashport, Ohio with her husband Paul. When not creating new worlds and romance, Kathi and her husband enjoy camping and going to auctions. She can also be seen at county fairs with her husband who is an artist and potter.

Her muse, a cross between Jimmy Stewart and Hugh Jackman, brings her stories to life for her readers in a way that has them coming back time and again for more. Her favorite genre is paranormal romance with a great deal of spice. You can visit Kathi online and drop her an email if you'd like. She loves hearing from her fans. aaronskiss@gmail.com.

Follow Kathi on her blog: http://kathisbartonauthor. blogspot.com/

www.ingramcontent.com/pod-product-compliance
Lightning Source LLC
Chambersburg PA
CBHW032135170626
46808CB00006B/2245